Lost Property

Robert John Goddard

DEDICATION

This book is dedicated to the 10,000,000 ethnic German civilians who were subjected to deportation, compulsory labour, expulsion and, in many cases, starvation and physical attack after World War 2. In total, at least 470,000 expellees may have died during these expulsions due to hypothermia, starvation and violence. The Red Cross and the German government cite a less verifiable 2,200,000 deaths.

ACKNOWLEDGMENTS

Having an idea for a novel and turning it into a cover
picture design is hard. I want to thank Andrea for
creating a wonderful cover for *Lost Property*.

andrea.price.concept

.

1

Wednesday – afternoon

Montgomery Bradley Brodnitz, known to his few friends as Monty, slammed on the brakes and came to a stuttering halt at the red light. He gunned the engine and thumped the palms of his hands on the wheel.

"For God's sake, what is it now?"

An articulated lorry rumbled across his path. The long line of cars suffocating in its cloud of diesel exhaust prompted Monty to pull the gear stick into neutral and tug at the handbrake. He rubbed at his forehead with thumb and forefinger. There was nobody there to listen to him. Not only did the stop-light remain stubbornly red, an orange light was now flashing the arrival of the tram. Monty breathed deeply, filled his cheeks with air and deflated them with a long and slow huff. Glancing at his watch, he shook his head and switched off the engine. He was wasting both fuel and his emotional energy. The refugees would have arrived by now. He had even left his city office early enough to arrive in *Tannenheim* with time to spare. Someone up there, he thought, just did not want him to be at the castle to witness this historic event.

Monty was not a man to use coarse language. He thought, and often said, that it betrayed a lack of intelligence and revealed a limited vocabulary. But he mouthed obscenities at World War 2 and the 2,000 tons of American and British aerial bombs and munitions that turned up each year in Germany. He even uttered a word he rarely used to describe the one bomb in particular that had prevented him from easing out of the city. He had been looking forward to seeing the refugees arrive but this unmentionable bomb had turned up on a building site near his shop.

There was, Monty knew, nothing earth shattering about digging up bombs from the war. In 2015, Germany was still contaminated with them. Barely a week went by without a German city street or a motorway being cordoned off or even evacuated due to an unexploded bomb. Monty had only a passing interest in bombs and things that happened far away and long ago but the one that they found on this historic day was in his city and was preventing him from getting home in time to see the arrival of his refugees. More than that, the unearthed bomb had a delay-action detonator. It was too dangerous to move and had to be defused where it was found. This meant that the city centre and the central station were closed, thus displacing the traffic to the outlying areas and turning quiet residential streets into busy roads. Monty had been stuck in town for a couple of hours.

Waiting for the tram to pass, Monty mentally prepared the letter he would send to the local authorities complaining about their inappropriate and hasty rebuilding of the city in the post-war years without taking the trouble to locate and dispose of this deadly legacy lying dormant beneath Germany's streets. Then he imagined himself writing an article complaining about the use of delay-action fuses. Originally designed to catch German emergency services out in the open, the ones that did not explode were an ever-present danger waiting for the slightest shift to detonate. This threat, just below the city streets, meant that one false move might bring the whole edifice crumbling down.

The tram waited at its stop while passengers got on and off. Monty almost missed Herr Vorberg. The man was in a suit and Monty had never seen him in anything other than a flour-covered striped apron while he distributed loaves, rolls and *Sacher* cake. His bakery was a hub for those who objected to the presence of refugees in the town and they gathered there to hear Herr Vorberg's views. Monty had heard him speak, his eloquence interrupted only by his baker's cough, on the necessity of keeping Germany for the Germans, of preserving German culture and warning against the dangers of Islam. Recently, Monty had seen him standing on the steps of the fountain in the square that marked the centre of their town. Monty assumed that Herr Vorberg's shop was no longer big enough to hold the crowd he was attracting. In the dark suit he was now wearing, he looked quite impressive.

Monty drummed his fingers on the steering-wheel and leaned forward to get a better view of the main street and the hills ballooning green over it. Night had yet to fall but the evening had announced its arrival and its intention of claiming the woodland. It was there in the slant of the sunlight fading through the trees. It was rolling out over the treetops and making the dark spaces between the trees darker.

Glancing at the main street in front of him, Monty saw that people seemed to be going about their lives as usual, ambling in and out of the post-office or the butcher's shop, some stopping to chat on the pavement.

The pack of motorcycles gleaming outside the bakery probably belonged to a group of bikers on their way up into the hills to enjoy a spin along the forest roads. They were nothing to worry about. If anything at all was dampening his spirits it was the thought that he should visit the doctor and have his heart looked at. He was sure it was nothing to worry about. A routine check-up was all that was needed.

The presence of *Tannenberg Schloss*, where the refugees were to be housed, was just visible on the crest of the hill as yellow/white splashes between the trees. Until recently, the *Schloss* had been invisible, its position in the foothills of the *Niebelungwald* marked by a golden cross that picked up the light from the setting sun. Seen as the gateway to the *Niebelungwald*, *Tannenheim Kreuz* was a landmark and its evening glow could be seen from roads all around. Behind the cross, the hills waved endlessly away, creating a microclimate where the air was always fresher and the sky a little bluer than the area bordering it.

Monty was able to see the castle now because the local authorities had seen fit to cut down the trees surrounding it when the decision to house refugees in the *Schloss* was made. Monty thought that the word "*Schloss*" was a misnomer. The building, its belvedere towers reminiscent of the Italian renaissance style, was more of a large house than a castle. It had been chosen to lodge the refugees because it was uninhabited, because access to motorised traffic was limited to one winding road and, perhaps, because it was almost invisible from the town below. Out of sight meant out of mind.

Monty switched on the engine as the tram whispered past. He pushed at the gear lever, let out the clutch, and the car moved forward. He rumbled over the tracks and headed up the main street remembering what his wife, Ingrid, had said about the local authority's decision. She had no patience for those *Idioten* in the town hall who had not learned from the past. She pointed out that the castle, in which the refugees were to be temporarily housed, was dangerously isolated.

"Isolation kills," Ingrid said. "They have learned nothing from our own history. In 1946 my parents and many other Sudetenland Germans were culturally, geographically and linguistically isolated and they paid a heavy price for it at the hands of the Czechs."

Monty wanted to interrupt and ask her what the alternatives were but Ingrid had been in no mood for further discussion on the topic.

There were several groups of people gathered outside the post-office, the bank and the supermarket. Some individuals were pointing their fingers in the direction of the castle and their interest prompted Monty to take his bike and go through the forest to see for himself what was going on. Maybe the refugees were yet to arrive. A roar from behind broke into his thoughts. The bikers were following him up the main street. He pulled over to let them pass and they accelerated up the road and into the *Niebelungwald*.

Tired and irritable, he emerged from his vehicle, disappeared through the front door of his house and came back out a few minutes later dressed for temperatures hovering around zero. With the pleasurable anticipation of freedom that his bicycle offered, he followed his breath to the shed, pulled out his bike and walked with it to the front gate. He was about to swing his leg over the seat and set off up the main road towards the castle when a tap on his shoulder and a voice in his ear stopped him in his tracks.

"*Herr Brodnitz. Ein Moment, bitte.*"

2

Wednesday – early evening

Herr Maier, Monty's neighbour, resembled a beyond-retirement-age gardener rather than the owner of the imposing white mansion on the other side of the street. When Monty had moved into his own house three years previously, he and Ingrid had done the "German thing" and introduced themselves to their neighbours. Over time, formality had given way to familiarity, the use of first names and the informal German *du* rather than the formal *Sie*. Not with Herr Maier. Only when the summer days were long and bright, did Monty discover that he had a first name at all. Frau Maier's exasperated and shrill "*Nein*, Wolfi" would fly across the road from their terrace in the sun. But use of the name "Wolfi" clearly belonged exclusively to his wife.

"*Bitte, ein Moment*," Herr Maier said again.

Monty took a step backwards. For Herr Maier, "*Ein Moment*" was a very flexible period of time that could drag on for an age and Monty wanted to see the arrival of his refugees before it got properly dark.

"I need your...," Herr Maier said in English, his

words stumbling, his hand twirling in writing movements.

"Signature?" Monty said.

"Correct. I need your signature."

It was then that Monty slid his eyes away from the shabby, worn-at-the-cuffs overcoat and focused on the clipboard his neighbour clasped in the fingers of a gloved hand. Monty angled his head and breathed in through his teeth. A jolt of pain shooting through his incisors reminded Monty of his dentist's warning concerning receding gums. He decided to make an appointment at the earliest opportunity. Monty said:

"What's it about this time?"

Herr Maier loved to collect signatures and present them to the local authorities although nothing was ever done about the dog poo, the street lighting or the motorcycle hooligans causing problems in the town centre.

"We must make our views heard," Herr Maier said. "The castle is no place for young men. What is more, there are reports that the *Fluchtlinge* will be given free access to the town. We must stop this madness now before it gets out of control. I'm sure you will support us, yes?"

He leaned backwards and opened his arms as if expecting applause. Monty said nothing. Herr Maier's complaint was not new. Many citizens of *Tannenheim* had expressed varying degrees of concern about the arrival of so many refugees in their town. At first, all that they could do was react to ever-changing events beyond Germany's borders and beyond the control of both the townsfolk and the national government. On 13 July, Hungary had erected razor wire on its border to try and stop the flow of displaced persons. Early September, pictures of three-year-old Aylan al-Kurdi, drowned during his Syrian family's attempt to reach Greece from

Turkey, had provoked a wave of public sympathy for refugees. On 7 September, Germany estimated that 800.000 people would be given shelter in 2015. A week later, the number was revised to 1000.000.

From the middle of September, the word "refugee" was on everyone's lips. They knew the people were coming but because numbers kept increasing nobody knew how many or their exact arrival date. The other word on everyone's lips was "*Angst*." Monty heard its sibilance in the post office, in the shops and the supermarket and whispered in the bank.

Just a few weeks previously, towards the end of October when the forest beyond the town was crisp and red, the local newspaper, *Tannenheimer Blatt*, announced that around 300 refugees would be temporarily housed in the empty castle on the hill overlooking the town. The word "temporary" brought little relief. They were to be "processed" in the town before moving on, therefore allowing fresh arrivals at regular intervals. The sibilant word "*Angst*" had been hissing ever since from lip to lip.

"It is a bit late for a petition, Herr Maier," Monty said. "The refugees are expected today."

"But, Herr Brodnitz, it is never too late to express ourselves."

Herr Maier's objection to lodging young men at the castle was shared by many people. Some did not want to see refugees in *Tannenheim* at all. Others, including Monty's wife, objected to the choice of the castle in particular. Monty suspected that this choice had roused something that dragged Ingrid back to a place in the past she was reluctant to visit.

"If we really care about our new arrivals and what is good for them," she said, "we should house them with families. These refugees need contact with local people. They need to be where the jobs are. And what about the children? They need to be educated. And Christmas is coming. What will that be like for them isolated in the castle?"

Ingrid was convinced that for all the talk of humanitarian aid, the plan was fundamentally flawed.

"They will be no better off than my parents were. Do you know what they said about the Sudetenland refugees in 1946? *Das graue Elend kommt* – the grey misery is coming. It will be no different in 2015 – worse if they are imprisoned in that castle."

Herr Maier belonged to those people who did not want refugees in the town at all but he was now fighting a rearguard action. He took a step forward and proffered the clipboard.

"*Bitte*," he said. "We have to think about our families - especially our children and grandchildren. We all know about their attitudes to women, but it's the threat of terrorists amongst them that frightens us the most. Who can say what a handful of maniacs will do with rucksacks, nails and some home-made explosive?"

Monty swung his bike round so that it stood between him and his neighbour. He disliked putting his name to anything but he especially disliked being associated with prejudice and fear.

"I really think it is too late to change anything," he said. But Herr Maier was not to be put off.

"And we should not forget the value of our houses. What would prospective buyers think if our streets were full of men with their women trailing behind them like cattle? Is that why you built your house here, Herr Brodnitz – to see its value tumble because of a bunch of foreigners?"

"I think that is an exaggeration, Herr Maier, if I may say so," Monty said, pushing his bike forward towards the kerb.

"Just think," Herr Maier went on indicating the house next door to Monty's. "Your forbears lived in that house, the Villa Rosa. What would they have thought about these people walking past their window?"

"Supportive, perhaps," Monty said, swinging his leg over the saddle, and finding the pedal with his foot. "They were Jews, remember?"

"That was different, Herr Brodnitz."

"Indeed, it was, Herr Maier. It is always different, isn't it?"

Monty was regretting his comment. Many of the townsfolk were revelling in the opportunity to show the world that their spirit of openness was a pleasing contrast to the evils of Nazism. By November most people had apparently become used to the idea of receiving refugees. It had surprised Monty how quickly the locals had adjusted to their imminent arrival and mobilised themselves. Collections for much needed shoes and clothes were set up and language courses were organised. In June, a handful of Syrian refugees were housed in an empty care home and they soon became a regular feature of town life.

"But the potential for conflict and violence is there, Herr Brodnitz. There are many people amongst us who are attracted by extreme German nationalist ideas. Only an excuse is needed."

Monty had to agree. Twenty-first century jihadist violence combined with pockets of deprivation in *Tannenheim* and the surrounding towns and villages provided receptive ears to anti-immigration groups. There was much support for German states that banned Muslim teachers from wearing headscarves and some attitudes had begun to harden.

"And these groups are getting more vocal in their opposition to Merkel's policy of openness."

Herr Maier had shifted his gaze to the right of Monty's right ear and a noise from behind made him turn. Herr Vorberg, the baker, was standing at his shoulder and stifling a cough with his hand. He cleared his throat and said:

"Maier is right. Were you not here when the *Front* marched through our town?"

Monty nodded.

"Indeed, I was, Herr Vorberg."

Several weeks previously members of the *Vaterlaendische Front*, or Fatherland Front, had marched through town with what looked like a band of Hells Angels riding shotgun. The *Vaterlaendische Front* had started in the spring as no more than a Facebook page. It had developed into a group with thousands of supporters, who were invited by the organiser to meet for "evening strolls" through German towns and cities to voice their opposition to the government's open-border policy. *"Wir sind das Volk"* some of the marchers shouted. This claim that "we are the people" was a choice of words designed to echo the protesters in East Germany before the Berlin Wall came down in 1989.

The baker raised a finger and shook it in Monty's direction.

"Do not ever underestimate the *"Sturmbannfuehrer,"* he warned. "We, the German people, once underestimated a corporal and we are paying for it to this day."

Monty knew that Herr Vorberg was referring to the driving force behind the *Front* – a shady individual known as the *Sturmbannfuehrer*. This, Monty knew, was a deliberate reference to a military rank equivalent to Major and had been used in several Nazi organisations, such as the SA and the SS. Fortunately, the *Vaterlaendische Front* seemed a harmless and diverse group.

"Those marchers seemed a reasonable group of people," Monty said. "I think you are worrying over nothing, Herr Vorberg."

Indeed, the march through *Tannenheim* had attracted everyone from a man calling for a ban on smoking in all public places to a woman campaigning against domestic violence. Monty noticed no grey-green SS combat uniforms amongst the strollers claiming that they were representing "the people." Those who marched through *Tannenheim* included wax-jacketed dog owners and their children, and sweat-shirted singles looking for love.

"Ach, you English, you understand nothing," Herr Vorberg said. His face had paled and his eyes flickered over Monty's face as if looking for the exact spot from which his lack of understanding had emerged. "If you had a history like ours, you would not be so relaxed about it all. And it is always the same: they bring drugs, diseases, and economic collapse. And if that is not enough, they take our women, too."

"You forget, Herr Vorberg, that I am half German, so I partly understand what you..."

But the baker had turned and was strutting away from Monty's attempt at a joke. In some ways, the man was right. Casting his mind back, Monty recalled that although many of the slogans held aloft by the "people" had held no interest for the children or dog walkers, others seemed to suggest that drug-dealing, diseases, economic collapse and breeding like rabbits were associated with foreigners in general and refugees in particular. Monty had also heard snatches of conversation concerning the need for tighter immigration controls, for keeping war refugees in their homelands, and for forcing foreigners in Germany to speak German at home.

"Forgive him, Herr Brodnitz," Herr Maier said. "He is merely exaggerating."

Monty was not so sure. He knew several people in *Tannenheim* with sympathies for the *Vaterlaendische Front.* Frau Werling, from the bookshop, was free with her comments. Most of them began with "I am not racist, but..." or "It is unfair to bunch us together with Nazis, but..." There was no question that there were neo-Nazis in the *Front* and the threat was strong enough to cause the Mayor of *Tannenheim* to urge local people not to join those whose "hearts were cold."

"*Dummkoepfe*," Ingrid had responded. "Words are not enough. Those dumb heads in the city office will need to bring the castle down, brick by brick, and rebuild it in the centre of town. If they don't do that, there will be trouble."

Monty zipped up his outer jacket and pressed down on the bicycle pedal.

"I wish you a good evening, Herr Maier."

"There will be trouble, Herr Brodnitz," Herr Maier said as Monty passed him.

It was too late to change anything.

"*Die Wuerfel sind gefallen*, Herr Maier," Monty said.

He paused on the corner of the street, checked for cars and pedalled up the main street towards the forest. Yes, Monty thought, *die Wuerfel sind gefallen* - the die was indeed cast.

3

Wednesday – evening

Monty arrived at the top of the main street and pushed off up the hill towards *Petershausen*. After a few metres, he swung onto an uphill track through the forest. Despite his appropriate clothing, Monty soon felt the cold and damp biting at his face and cutting through the outer jacket. He had expected more from a garment named *Chainmale.* The brand promised protection and Monty felt a rise of pity for Ingrid who had been fooled into buying it for his 63rd birthday.

The *Schloss* was about ten minutes away and *Tannenheim* owed its existence to ancient suppliers of the castle. Bread, meat and other necessities had been transported along small paths through the woodland by the butcher, the baker and the candlestick maker for at least 800 years. Monty was now very familiar with these old routes, as were the multitude of other bikers and walkers who made their way up to the castle and beyond to explore the 3,500 square kilometres of the *Niebelungwald.*

The original castle had been built in 1230 and had the

dubious distinction of being the first castle in Germany to be destroyed by canon fire. The new castle had been erected in the middle of the 19th century on the ruins of the previous one and the old pink stones rose from the ground and gripped the fresh stone-work like gums grip teeth. The castle had been in the hands of a local aristocratic family for years but World War 1 and the Verdun battle had taken not only the heir to the estate but also his two brothers. Consequently, the property was taken over by the county in 1928 and had been adopted by the Nazi regime as a training centre for the young women of the German Women's Guild. From 1946 until 2010 it was used as a teachers' training college. The castle had been abandoned until the local authorities decided it was the ideal place to house the arrivals Monty had come to see.

It was not yet dark but, whatever the time of day, there was always something of the night in the forest - even at the height of summer when trees screened the light with their leaves. Monty did not turn on his lamps. On all but the darkest nights, it was fascinating what you saw once your eyes adjusted. He would often stop by the side of the path and let the stars and the moon light up the badgers, the hedgehogs, the mice and the foxes. He had even seen wild boar in these woods.

Monty changed down to a lower gear. He breathed deeply. Air was like fuel to him. *Take a deep breath, Monty; relax the hands and push down hard on the pedals.* His legs felt light, responsive and strong. *Take another deep breath, Monty - head down, eyes on the narrow track, keep a slow but steady pace.* There was a sharp pain in his knee. *Nothing new there. Ignore it and it will go away.* Another deep breath. He felt the beat of his heart in his neck, sometimes appearing to pause on a knife edge before thumping forward again. *Breathe, Monty, breathe. Change down to first gear and relax.*

After 10 minutes, the outline of the cross materialised and the path veered off to the right to begin its long circuit through the forest to the back of the castle. He paused to get his breath and, loosening his scarf, he swung round in the saddle. He was alone except for the sound of his breathing and the familiar sense of anticipation gripping at his bowels. This feeling, that something was about to happen, always accompanied him at night into the heart of the forest. Monty shook his head and told himself to calm down. Apart from boars protecting their young, there was nothing to worry about. Fear of forests was a response learned in childhood through stories of ogres, dragons or wolves stalking their victims and gobbling them up.

Monty lifted his head and listened. He hardly made out the sound of distant traffic but whoever had written the words to the Christmas carol "Silent Night" had clearly never been in a forest as night came. The first bats were zigzagging over his head and beneath them the creatures that hid all day were now emerging to feast, fight and kill. He heard them sliding, falling, scuttling and jumping and the air was alive with squeaks, rustles, grunts and cries of terror and of death.

Pushing down on the pedals again, Monty cast his thoughts forward to see the refugees in his mind's eye. They were black and white and dusty with frightened eyes, their belongings stuffed in wooden suitcases with leather handles or dangling on the end of sticks that rested on their shoulders. Monty paused again and shook this vision away. Clearly, his response to the word "refugee" had been strongly influenced by news footage of that time and by Ingrid's tales of ethnic Germans thrown out of their homelands in Sudetenland following the end of European hostilities in May 1945. She would often go for months at a time without saying a word on the topic but just the other day, and quite out of the blue, she had said to him:

"They were full of pent up rage."

The word "they," out of context and arriving suddenly like that, sent Monty's imagination whirling.

"Who? The VF marchers?"

Ingrid neither confirmed nor rejected Monty's query but followed the line of her own thoughts.

"The Czechs. After the war."

"Ah," said Monty, concluding that the imminent arrival of refugees in their community had, with Ingrid, sparked off thoughts of her parents and what had happened to them at the end of World War 2.

"Rage at what?"

"The world? Some personal problem? The war? It was all taken out on us Germans between May and August 1945. And as if Oma Gretl and Opa Siegfried had anything to do with it, yet alone mum and dad."

"Did nobody try and stop the violence?"

"In 1945? No. Some Czech politicians encouraged it and local officials acted accordingly. They allowed armed volunteers to implement the orders along with the army. Several thousand Germans were murdered during the process, and many more died on the road back home."

"But Waltraud and Kurt left in 1946, didn't they?"

"Mum and dad? Yes, they were lucky. In 1946, the expulsions were better controlled. Train transport was organised with food and basic medical support. Eight hundred thousand were deported to the Soviet zone. My Oma Gretl and mum, my Opa Siegfried, his wife Traudel and dad were among them. Mum was 10 years old at the time and dad was twelve."

Monty shook his head again and this immediate image disappeared in a cloud of summer dust. Time had passed, he reminded himself. The roads covered by his imagined post-war refugees had long since been metalled. The colourless television images of the displaced children of his childhood memory no longer tramp-tramped nursing blister and belly till arrival at their own castles in the sky.

What was more, Monty liked to think that the world in 2015 was a friendlier and more caring place than it had been in 1946. He imagined the new arrivals being greeted now by the Mayor of *Tannenheim*. There would be no bundles of rags here. Hands would be shaken, speeches given, opportunities for self-promotion taken. After that, he expected to hear shouts and sounds of merriment and relief. He contemplated mingling with the crowd, welcoming them himself and joining them to discuss the two things they would have in common - their foreignness and the fact that his own father had been a refugee in 1939. It even occurred to him that they might have a need for some of the electronic goods that stuffed his shop - endless mobile phones and tablets to contact those left behind at home.

But Monty did not see or hear anything until he rounded a tight bend in the track. At a distance of about 100 metres he noticed that the area to the side of the castle was lit up. There was something not quite right about what he saw. The 2-metre-high fence was bathed in light so intense it seemed that an enthusiastic electrician had overdone the neon lights and they were now overheating, the smoke passing like clouds over the portable toilets lining the perimeter fence.

Monty was sweating now and a breeze had picked up and rustled the leaves in the trees. He told himself he was not ready for the castle just yet, was not ready to meet and talk to the refugees. He needed a few minutes alone to catch his breath and calm himself. He listened again to the sounds of the forest but a roar like that coming from a football crowd reached out from the direction of the castle. Something was wrong. The hot and cold feeling in his stomach confirmed that something was wrong. That something had set his adrenaline pumping.

Monty pressed down harder on the pedals, the rear tyre sliding in the mud and nearly throwing him off. When he regained his balance the full force of collective hate deafened him, numbed his mind. He stood astride his bike - frozen. He hardly breathed. He could do nothing but watch.

"Scum, go home," someone shouted.

His heart thumped in his neck and then paused like bated breath - a particularly disturbing pause that left him breathless. It seemed that the shout was directed at the building. People were throwing stones. Others launched what looked like fireworks at a bus full of people. Some people were screaming. Then everyone screamed. A mass of demonstrators, several in Klu-Klux-Klan-ish white robes, waved the German flag.

"*Sieg Heil.*"

"*Heil* Hitler."

There were people on the ground by the bus. They were coughing and bleeding. A mob surged forward. They backed off at the fire, disappeared in fumes wafting from the burning upholstery. Frenzied attackers moved forward. They raised metal bars. Surely, they were not going to hit people lying on the ground?

No, no, someone stop it.

There was a smash of breaking glass. There was a crash when people hit the sides of the bus. Tyres were slashed. There was a shout and a shattering of glass. And in the intermittent and flashing light, there was the figure in a white robe throwing back his hood. There was another flash and then another - and then the face - out of place, an impossible person - and then he was laughing.

No, it can't be... It can't be...

19

Monty threw himself sideways, brought his hands to his eyes and rubbed at them as though ridding them of the image he had seen. His heart was ticking like a sick clock, erratic against his sternum. Throwing the bike round he headed off. Pedalling was somehow therapeutic. How long had he stood watching that barbarity? He was shaking in time to his fluttering and thumping pulse. He could not get away from the burning. Its smell was following him down the hill.

It can't be him. It can't be him.

A smudge of light appeared through the trees and Monty pushed down harder on the pedals but the smell must have got into his *Chainmale* jacket. He could not shake it off any more than he could shake off the sweat that was rolling down his back. He sailed through the forest to the sound of sirens and bells ringing in his head. He skidded to a halt, covered his ears to keep the sounds at bay.

"It can't be him, can it?

He was unable to get rid of the smell and nor could he stop the feeling of something shifting in his head, a profound shift in consciousness, an intense dissatisfaction with himself and an urge to do something about it.

The next few minutes were wiped clean. In his memory, he came to life again in his house.

Yes, it could be him.

He went straight for the drinks cabinet and threw down a very large scotch before looking through the doorway and the stairs leading up to his son's room.

4

Wednesday - evening

Monty caught sight of his slim body reflected in the window. Fully aware of what he was about to do, he did not allow his eyes to linger on this reflection. Somehow, awareness of his intentions changed his hawkish nose and the wavy "huge" hair from being rakish and charming to something altogether different, something best described by the words "spiv" "treacherous" and "dishonourable." He did not even want to imagine what his father would have said - but he did.

Monty allowed his hand to hover by the light switch but dropped his arm and walked through the door, into the darkened corridor and placed his foot on the first step. He liked the darkness. Under its cover, his troubled soul was invisible even to himself and it gave him the illusion that nothing had changed, that despite what he had just seen at the castle, everything remained, and would remain, the same.

At the top of the stairs he felt his way along the corridor, past his office and the master bedroom. He came to an abrupt halt under the short flight of stairs that led into Julian's room. Someone had shifted the large wooden box containing the Christmas decorations and Monty had walked right into it. It was a bit early to think about Christmas, Monty thought while contorting his face and waiting for the pain in his little toe to subside. Then he reconsidered. It was never too early for Ingrid to plan for anything. He was about to give the offending box a retaliatory kick but stopped himself. The box had a leather strap for a handle. There was an address written in old German script in one corner. The letter "N" for the Czech *Nemec* - meaning "German" - had been painted in the opposite corner. This box had once been a suitcase, a piece of luggage now containing the memories of Ingrid's mother and father who, as children, had been forced out of their homes in the Sudetenland. A barrier, more than darkness, prevented him from further movement. But it was not this relic from the past that put the brakes on him. It was the memory of his old school motto that stopped him from committing the unspeakably boorish act of searching his own son's room.

Modeste, Strenue, Sancte – in these extraordinary circumstances this motto was somehow insufficient and was failing him. But "be modest, be thorough, and pursue righteousness" were not commandments that would cave in without a struggle. Their power and stamina forced Monty to step backwards as if something unpleasant or unexpected had appeared at his feet. He had been well into his fifties before he fully understood the extent to which his personal values had been shaped by those of his old school - Wimbledon Grammar School for Boys. A creak from the floor made him turn his head. He was half expecting to see a prefect with mortar board standing in the doorway, his gown languid over his shoulders and his huge mouth berating.

"You are breaking the rules, Brodnitz. Remember the pursuit of righteousness."

Monty shook his head and although the apparition dissolved into the darkness, his warnings still rang in Monty's head. The pursuit of righteousness, according to Wimbledon Grammar, meant an acceptance of the school's organisation, the maintenance of discipline by the older boys and the minimal interference from teachers. Righteousness meant acceptance of the "fagging" system, group conformity and loyalty. Righteousness meant accepting initiation rites and bullying without complaint so that boys would become men and leaders of men. Righteousness was good manners, honesty and openness, self-sufficiency and using your own initiative. Heresy was dishonesty and bad manners, and above all, "snitching on" or betraying other boys to the prefects or teachers. So, Monty asked himself, what was he doing here about to break the rules? Looking through your son's belongings hardly conformed to an action that was in accordance with the accepted standards of morality and justice as expounded by Wimbledon Grammar School for Boys.

Feeling like a morally inferior and shabby being, Monty walked up the short flight of steps, paused at the half-open door and peered into Julian's room. In the semi-darkness, it was very much like the room had been when Julian was 10 years old. As a rule, Julian only came home at weekends these days. He was nineteen and studying in the city where Monty worked. The main difference between the room now and the room as it had been was the cool glow of light marking the presence of the computer, the phone and clock.

Immediately to Monty's left was the bookcase he had put together himself. About twenty paperbacks stood on it, lay against each other, casually discarded by their owner and left like that by a caring mother not wishing to disturb. In the summer months, the wind blew through the open window and the books stood fluttering in the breeze as if advertising their content to whoever was present. Monty was not staring at these books now. He was intrigued to see a volume that had detached itself from the others. Its spine had buckled and it had fallen flat on its side as though rejected, pushed away like a leper. He recognised it immediately. It was Julian's diary. Monty stepped forward, hand outstretched and ready to pounce. He came to a halt as if he had bumped into the suitcase again.

How can you do this, Monty? You are about to spit on your wife and rape her feelings. Not only that, what you are about to do is against your own moral code and one that has served you so well.

Monty backed away.

No, Monty, you have to go through with this. This is your son we are talking about here. You have to know the truth. You have a right to know it and the uncertainty would be intolerable.

So, Monty laid his old school motto on the floor, stepped to one side of himself and walked into the room hoping Ingrid would never discover what he had done. If she did, she would never forgive him, and marriage breakdown and divorce might follow. Given Ingrid's background, Monty thought, nobody would blame her.

In early eighties East Berlin, she had been a hippy rebel - outrageous clothes, drugs, defiant attitude, the works. She clearly did not fit the profile of a good socialist citizen. She thought that was why she caught the eyes of the *Stasi*. She had kept her nose clean, she said, by working in a *Trabant* factory, but she never voted, which was, of course, mandatory. Then, in early 1986 she began to protest against authoritarian government by putting up posters. The night she was caught, there were so many police around she knew she had been betrayed by someone. When informers were watching you, she said, they wrote down everything: when you left home in the morning, what time you caught the tram, where you were going, who you came into contact with. She didn't recognise herself in her file. The informers depicted her as evil. Everything she did, however innocent, was loaded with suspicion.

In the prison, they kept asking what group Ingrid belonged to because they wanted her to betray the leaders. They could not believe she would do something like that on her own and act on her own conscience. She was released 8 months later and expatriated to West Germany in 1987. They threatened her with a longer term in jail if she did not go.

After the Berlin Wall came down in 1989, Ingrid decided to read her own *Stasi* file but it was not until January 1992 that the *Stasi* Archives in Berlin were officially opened to the public and to former East Germans, like Ingrid, curious to see their files and anxious to know who had betrayed them.

Ingrid's file contained reports submitted by more than twenty different *Stasi* agents and informers. The most complete reports came from three informers code-named, Peter, Donald and Eva. These reports included full accounts of her anti-Government activities, as well as intimate details of her private life.

Monty moved smoothly through the room. He searched Julian's book shelves, his desk and its drawers and poked his nose into plastic bags, toys and books. He knew exactly what he was looking for. When Monty had started his job in lost property in 1986, he had come across all sorts of oddities. Many of these were reported to the police, for example, the toy baby rabbit concealing a Smith and Wesson revolver, the prosthetic leg containing packets of heroin, the football stuffed with cocaine and the child's toy rattling with ecstasy tablets.

The fact was that illegal drugs had never formed part of Monty's world. While growing up in the sixties, Monty was aware of drugs like hashish, cocaine and LSD but he never considered using them. To Monty's way of thinking, and his father's teaching, drugs were linked to top Nazi leaders and undesirables from the secondary modern school. Drugs did not conform to the pursuit of righteousness. They were against the law and, therefore, associated with underhand dealings in alleyways and with criminals and other such damaged people.

Over the years, Monty had become adept at distinguishing washing powder from heroine, sweets from ecstasy tablets and herbal tea from hashish. Any crystalline substance which turned up in mislaid nappies or briefcases meant an instant call to the police. He did not consider himself an expert but he learned that the purest heroin was a fine white powder. He also learned that if it was gray, brown or black it had been cut with additives like sugar or caffeine.

When he had finished with the shelves and the drawers, Monty sat down on the swivel chair and logged on to his son's email provider. While waiting, he caught sight of his own reflection in the computer screen but it was not him staring back. It was the image of a perfect stranger and the stranger was allowing him to do things he was unable to do as Mongomery Bradley Brodnitz. While this image searched, rifled, read and perused his son's internet sites, Monty imagined the report he would have written for the *Stasi* dated, 26 November 2015.

> "8.00 - Observation of J's room. Small bags of brownish-green leaves on the bookshelf and chunks of a powdery brown substance in the drawers of J's desk. Discarded cigarette papers and filters found

on desk. 8.20 - Bags found in J's childhood teddy. One bag contained a crystalline powder. Other bag contained crystalline chips and chunks. 8.40 – Gay magazines found in J's drawers. Examination of J's computer reveals extensive viewings of gay sites, and sites on how to make Molotov cocktails. Evidence of close contact on email and Facebook with members of a group called the *Vaterlaendische Front*. Evidence of good relationship with the VF's leader – the *Sturmbannfuehrer*. 8.50 - Observations terminated."

When Ingrid had read her own *Stasi* file way back in 1992, she had only one initial question. Who were Peter, Donald and Eva? Ingrid's reading of her files left only one possible, terrible conclusion. It was a moment she later described as "life destroying" - that moment she realized that those who had betrayed her to the *Stasi* were her brother Dieter and her parents, Kurt and Waltraud.

5

Friday – late afternoon

Monty drummed his fingers on the arm of his chair. He was waiting for Julian to walk through the door. The thought of questioning his son had sent him into a tailspin. He raised his hand and brought it down with a thwack on his thigh. Monty had experience of getting teenagers out of bed, ensuring they did their homework and ate properly but dealing with a criminal act was foreign territory and way beyond a simple father-son issue. He took a deep breath and blew out his cheeks. He had had two days to consider but his mind was still blank. He shook his head. There was only one answer to his indecisiveness, and the violence he had witnessed at the castle was exposing it. He was weak and indecisive, a man his own father would have been ashamed of.

Slipping his hands into the pockets of his trousers, he stretched his legs and crossed his ankles with a scissor kick. Attempting to refocus his thoughts he looked through the glass wall of the sitting room and concentrated on blinds. When he and Ingrid designed this house, they had wanted as much light as possible. Since witnessing the attack at the castle, Monty was having doubts about the floor to ceiling glass. The absence of curtains or blinds made him feel vulnerable and exposed to an outside world that would judge him to be an inadequate father. He wondered where this vacillating ditherer had been hiding all these years. Perhaps it was a genetic problem and caused by an abnormality in the genome. Had indecision been lurking since birth and waiting for the right time to declare itself?

The sight of the composter consoled him somewhat. Monty was not displeased to see its steam rising into the late November dusk, thicken over the wall and merge with the mist to hide his house from prying eyes.

Monty contemplated the drinks table, was sorely tempted to bury his self-disgust in a large whisky. But he stayed in the chair. There was no need to add to the ageing process by overdoing it on the alcohol. He had already noticed that his thighs no longer filled out and shaped his trousers and his skin was puckering around the mouth and hanging kimono-like from under his triceps. On top of that, his blood pressure was a touch too high and his heart had been doing odd things recently. The doctors might be able to help him with his heart and blood but ageing and genetic disorders like indecision and prevarication were beyond the help of modern medicine.

It occurred to him his dilemma might well be connected to age and its tendency to whimsical judgements. In his twenties he had not agonised over silly things like decisions. He knew where he was going and how he was going to get there. Everything he did had been based on pragmatism and self-interest. It had certainly been self-indulgence, albeit of a harmless variety, that had taken him from Wimbledon to Central

London to study the History of Art. He had given no thought to the future or what he would do with the qualification when he got it. At the time, he simply enjoyed being with objects of beauty. Towards the end of his course he learned how to make coherent *curriculum vitae* in order to get a job. He had no scruples about changing "self-indulgence" into a "passion" for antiques and he got a job in London with an established antiques dealer. In the first few years, he learned inventory systems, bookkeeping methods, and payment and cash-flow. What was more, he increasingly helped in both face-to-face dealings with clients and in valuations. He spent long hours inspecting pieces, consulting with other dealers and researching histories. The hours were long and the pay was pitiful.

Monty slipped his hands from his pockets and clasped them behind his head. Apart from these revelations of personal weakness, this Friday afternoon was like any other Friday afternoon in autumn - so normal it seemed that nothing had happened - nothing at all. Only 48 hours had passed since the attack and the town was still vitalised by it. Monty sensed this energy in the people that passed by outside. Actually, it was only the tops of heads he saw bobbing above the wall but the heads seemed about to leap up and declare themselves with a shriek before being struck with a club from a Punch or a Judy.

So, what had happened to the man who had made a snap decision to do the Distance Learning MBA at Manchester Business School? Where was the man who made a series of other timely decisions that helped him establish a network with fellow professional antique dealers? Had this man taken early retirement? He was still very active in 1985 when a confident Monty so lightly made a decision that changed his life. At the time, he felt he was doing something on a whim but he knew now, in retrospect, that his yearning for independence was expected at that stage of his career. In 1985 he was thirty-three, had established his own network of contacts, gained useful and usable experience and he had matured as a man and as dealer. More importantly, he knew that salaries did not rise beyond that current point unless you started your own business. The surprising opportunity-of-a-lifetime offer came from a place he had always wanted to visit - Germany.

The offer was not entirely a logical progression for an antiques dealer but Monty had jumped at the chance. When he was asked later why he had taken a job in the Lost Property business he sometimes said that such a position enabled him to satisfy his passion for recycling and saving the planet. At other times he emphasised the fact that he had always wanted to travel or work abroad. If he was feeling cynical, which was a mood or stance he increasingly allowed himself, he simply stated that career development was merely another word for blundering from one position to another and driven by boredom. Morose and depressed in the sitting-room Monty now reflected that never, in those early days, had he mentioned the pull of his roots and the urge to visit the place in which his father, Max, had grown up.

With nothing else to occupy his thoughts, he considered sneaking upstairs to check his son's room for signs of his own treacherous entry two nights previously. Julian would be home soon and Monty did not want him discovering his father's fingerprints on the wall or scuffs from his shoes on the skirting boards. Perhaps, Monty had disturbed the edges of the rug or had left other tell-tale signs of intrusion that he was unaware of.

Monty pushed out both arms and, stretching them above his head, threw his legs outwards again and lay back on the sofa. If he sat there much longer, Ingrid would be home and he would be prevented from creeping up the stairs and going through with this cowardly task.

Is this what it comes to, Monty, old boy? Your personal integrity and righteousness falling away like rotting teeth?

Maybe, Ingrid would be better off with someone else, Monty thought, someone more upright, honourable and decisive - someone who could deal with the challenge presented by his son, someone like his own father, perhaps. A colleague had recently commented that Monty had been lucky to find a woman such as Ingrid. Monty now assumed that his colleague was suggesting that Monty was undeserving, that Ingrid was, in some way, unlucky in finding Monty. And if he were undeserving was that because of his lack of moral fibre now exposing itself at this difficult time? Or perhaps his colleague had been referring to Monty's age and its tendency to dither, hover, complain and do nothing. Monty was about to reach the age of sixty-four. His hair could still be described as "huge" and "sweeping," a hangover from the eighties even if the hair was no longer all-covering. Yes, the hair still emerged from head, ears and nose in a sprouting of grey power and fertility, but it was not helping him decide how to deal with his son.

A familiar figure appeared on the pavement. Ingrid was standing at their wrought-iron gate and fumbling in her bag for the door key. Was he lucky that he had found her? He immediately realised how difficult it was to see her as others did. "Taking someone for granted" was the expression that came to mind. After 22 years, that really should not have surprised him. Monty barely gave a thought to those superficial relics of her hippy days, the jeans and the long, greying pony tail. He was focused instead on what other people would not notice: the fumbling hand, her head flicking from side to side, the nervous glances down the street and into a past that had been following her since her student days in East Berlin.

Monty thought that those familiar nervous glances had assumed a quality of something not quite under her control - a sort of permanent nervous tic, and it forced Monty to disregard that ageing-hippy exterior and to see something more fundamental, something that raised his protective instincts. Monty supposed that if he also spent time incarcerated in a prison perched on a hill his life would change forever. Eight months behind the walls of *Hohenseck* - the medieval fort used as a jail for political dissidents in the DDR - would leave their mark on anyone. Recent attempts to recycle *Hohenseck*, and to sell authentic jail experiences to tourists eager to touch reality in East Germany's largest women's prison, were met with an unusual and disapproving silence from Ingrid. She rarely discussed politics these days. This reticence, Monty supposed, resulted from an upbringing in East Germany where politics had been a taboo topic in the same way that masturbation had been taboo when he was growing up in England in the fifties and sixties. Not a happy comparison, Monty thought. Masturbation had not resulted in a prison sentence even though the Catholic Church had condemned it as a grave moral disorder. Perhaps he was damaged, even as a child. Maybe, after 22 years, Ingrid had looked right through him and now saw him as the sham he was.

Just recently she had made a comment that disturbed him. While in prison, she and hundreds of other women were forced to make garments for a well-known clothes manufacturer in the West. Ingrid cast a scathing eye over Monty and added that these were garments that Monty himself might have bought and worn while listening to songs by Morrissey. It was the bitterness in her voice that shook Monty. He had never heard it before - not even when they first met in 1993 and they had shared their life stories.

Ingrid's story began and ended with her family. She, her brother, Dieter, and her parents, had been very close, she said. Brother and sister played in a band together during the early eighties. In 1993, just before she met Monty, she decided to go back east and confront her family about their betrayal of her to the *Stasi*. Her parents had refused to see her but she surprised Dieter at his house. He looked nervous, but they both pretended to be delighted to see each other. They opened a bottle of *Rotkaeppchen*. When she raised her glass, she looked through the sparkling wine at his distorted face and told him she knew who had informed on her. Dieter was shocked, but said he did not feel guilty. If they had not been keeping an eye on her, he said, she would have gone to prison anyway and for a longer period of time. Her family had done a good job, he claimed, of protecting her.

"That was what they all claimed," Ingrid said.

For a person who maintained that prison had taught her patience, forgiveness and fortitude there was more than a touch of resentment in Ingrid's voice. But Monty sometimes forgot to remember that after that meeting with Dieter, Ingrid never saw her brother again and never tried to contact her parents. Monty also forgot to remember that prison had not only taken away her freedom but also something far more significant.

"It's beyond me, Monty," she said. "I just haven't been able to shed a tear since."

This dismayed Monty. Ingrid was not a marble statue, unable to feel anything, but he felt that weeping might set her free and let her move on from her experiences in prison. It was revealing, Monty thought, that the most positive expressions she had used to describe prison life were the adjective "stressful" and the phrase "subject to strict controls." With regard to other prisoners she would smile and dismiss them with words like "abusive" and "violent." Nonetheless, Ingrid delighted in telling him about some of the extraordinary people prison life brought her into contact with. Some of these demonstrated a degree of compassion, patience and kindness in the face of adversity that inspired her. She had seen prisoners, some of whom had committed terrible crimes, take control of their lives by refusing to be the victim and developing the potential to do good. It had been a powerful experience for her to discover that by refusing to assume a "poor-me" attitude and taking responsibility for herself, she did not have to allow a prison sentence to define the rest of her life.

Monty watched Ingrid mentally slap herself, swing on her sensible medium-height shoes and trip off towards the main street with the pony tail swinging behind her. He guessed she had forgotten to stop off at the supermarket. Maybe she needed some beer for Julian. A heavy odour of burning, drifting under his nostrils, forced Monty to his feet. He dashed into the kitchen but his pasta bake displayed no signs of charring - it was sizzling away nicely.

He stood stock still a moment before rushing to the staircase and climbing the stairs to his son's room.

6

Friday – early evening

Monty dithered in the doorway and stared into his son's room as if it were a pit of evil. In a sense, Monty thought, it was just that, or at best, the room reached out to the Mr Hyde in his nature while Dr Jekyll looked on helplessly. Monty looked down at his hands. He was holding them together, palms upwards and cupped as if about to receive Holy Communion. Even at this time of moral qualms the desire to go into Julian's room and rifle through his possessions again was so powerful.

Perhaps he was fundamentally rotten. Perhaps the years had stripped away the leaves until he was laid bare as the poor father and coward he was. The problem lay with him - not in his son or in some bad gene. The values he had learned at school, the example set by his father's actions and values - these had provided nothing but a veneer he had been wearing all these years and now, at this time of crisis, he was unable to live up to them.

He backed away, his eyes now accustomed to the

darkness and his ears to the stillness. He negotiated the downward steps and made his way along the corridor, past the master bedroom and his office. With one hand firmly placed on the banister, Monty stepped down the stairs and paused on the landing. He gazed through the window and towards the trees that separated his new-build house from the Italianate Villa Rosa next door. The villa itself was just visible as a glowing patch of yellow light in an upstairs window. Against the light Monty saw the birch trees, upturned witches' brooms swaying in a quickening wind.

When the villa's owner, Peter Lutz, had decided to put a part of his garden up for sale, Monty and Ingrid had been able to buy the land and build their house on it. The day they moved in, Monty glanced up to the sky and bursting with pride he had said to the clouds:

Look, dad, I am now a success and I am bringing you back home – home to the town you were born in and to the house where you grew up.

The villa had been built around 1880 by his paternal great grandfather, Rudi, and was named after Max's grandmother. Rudi had clearly been influenced by the elaborate window crowns and pediments that he had seen in Italy but the Italianate style was also, perhaps unknown to him, a part of a shift in taste that wanted architectural forms reflecting an earlier period of history.

Despite the fact that Peter Lutz had sold off large chunks of garden, his house still stood like a palace in substantial grounds. The outhouses, once stables no doubt, edged the curved driveway. Built at a time before the need for barbed wire or electrified fencing the house was protected by wrought-iron railings. Outside the massive gates the pavement was stamped with evidence that betrayal of friends and family, their political persuasion or their religion was not an activity restricted to the DDR. The Nazis had also encouraged it and the results were the five *Stolperstein* in the pavement at the gate. These raised trip stones were arranged in a triangle. At the apex was the name of Monty's paternal grandmother, Ida Brodnitz. Under the name was the legend: *Geb. Benjamin 1898. Deportiert 1942. Ermordert 16.09.1942 in Theresienstadt.* Inscribed on the other four stones were the names of his grandfather, two uncles and a young child. The date and place of their deaths bore witness to the fate of almost all of Max's family.

But Max, at least, had set a good example and acted decisively. He got out of *Tannenheim* in 1939 when he was nineteen. He fled to Britain and later joined the British army. After the war, he lived and worked in England where Monty was born in 1952. Monty's father had named his son Bradley Montgomery in honour of the two men he had admired most - Lieutenant General Omar Bradley of the US First Army and General Bernard Montgomery of the British Second Army during the D-Day operations.

Monty lingered awhile on the landing and stared at nothing in particular while telling himself that he had no right to be associated in any way with such illustrious soldiers. His father had made a mistake. While Bradley and Montgomery were strong and brave, Monty was weak and prevaricating. The fact that it had taken him thirty-three years to come to the country of his forbears was just another example of his indecisiveness.

Monty considered for a moment longer before taking two steps down the stairs. There was another way of looking at it. The delay in coming to Germany might well have been due to his father. Somehow, Monty thought, his father's death in 1985 had freed him up, given him permission to visit his roots. He meditated a moment longer until a sound from the street - the whistling wind or the siren from an emergency vehicle -

brought him back to himself.

Monty swivelled on his heel and clipped down the stairs and into the light-splattered entrance hall. He saw shapes through the glass of the entrance door and heard familiar voices from the pavement. Ingrid and Julian were conversing with Herr Maier. The voices came to him as a rise and fall of tones interspersed with silences as they no doubt looked at the pavement with appropriately sad faces and said there were no words to describe the terrible attack and violence at the castle, the ensuing fire and those terrible injuries - and here in *Tannenheim* of all places.

No doubt Herr Maier had told them that such violence had not occurred in *Tannenheim* since 1945 when a detachment of young German soldiers, eager for glory before the war ended, came down from the hills and arrived in the main street in full battle dress while the American occupiers were celebrating in the bars and restaurants. The Germans managed to create mayhem before the GIs knew what was happening. But under the leadership of a tall Texan wielding a Colt 45 with an ivory handgrip, the Americans rallied. The results of the ensuing fire fight were still visible on Monty's garden wall as a row of chips from the bullets of a German *Schmeisser* MP40. Monty found these scars from the past faintly moving. For him, dead things, ordinary things, had the longest memories. Beneath their stillness, they were alive with the events they had seen and the brave people who had set those events in motion.

Monty lingered in the centre of the entrance hall, waiting for Herr Maier to go home and release Ingrid and Julian from his grip. Perhaps it was this fascination for the ordinary that had persuaded him to take up the position in Germany. It was the *Deutsche Bahn* which helped kick-start Monty's unusual venture after the railway operator put its lost property organisation out to tender. A German friend and colleague of Monty's had won the bid with his *Fundsachenverkauf* or "Lost Property Sale" and he invited Monty to come to Germany to run it. The sky was the limit, he added by way of temptation.

Monty accepted immediately and acted quickly. He enrolled on an intensive German course and struggled through the complexities of the language's grammar. He found that the study of Latin - provided so many years previously by Wimbledon Grammar in the shape of "Harry" Hathaway, the Latin master - an immense help in coming to terms with German datives, accusatives and genitives and their endings. Towards the end of his course he even felt confident enough to bemoan the absence of the ablative and the vocative. His old school had done a good job - *quod erat demonstrandum.*

By the middle of 1986, armed with a very good knowledge of grammar, Monty drove out to Germany. This new departure was, he told everyone, an entry into the world of Recycling Management. Anything lost by travellers through Germany would probably pass through Monty's hands. In 2015, after nearly 30 years, and nearing retirement age, Monty thought himself to be successful. But now he was torturing himself with doubts. True, he had built his own house.

Yes, but on the misfortune of others, Monty.

And he had sent his son, Julian, to the international school and he had managed to put away enough money for his retirement.

Paid for by the lost property of others, old boy.

What was more, he was now able to take Friday afternoons off and leave his business in the care of a recently recruited Office Manager.

Although it still tickled Monty when he reflected that his success was down to all those people who continued their journeys temporarily timeless, bookless, keyless, hatless and short-sighted, Monty liked to think that at least the absent-minded could relax in the knowledge that their lost possessions would enjoy a new lease of life.

And you did not steal them, did you, Monty. Come on, man, get a grip.

Indeed, he received 8000 objects from his partners at airports, the postal service and the railways every month. The shelves of his shop were full of boxes stuffed with glasses, watches, keys, laptops, books, mobile phones and items of clothing. Travellers were free to claim their belongings and many did. They had up to 3 months to claim their lost property and after that time, Monty was able to do what he wanted with it. For sale at that very moment, he had a necklace worth 18000 Euros and a watch valued at 35000. Some items were put up for sale at auction. Others were sold online. In the back room of Monty's shop, technicians were always hard at work. The laptops and phones had their memories wiped before being restored. Specialists were always brought in to repair jewellery and new pieces were sometimes made from broken bracelets, single earrings and watch straps.

Another passing blue light flickered through the hallway and a distant siren wailed in unison with the church bells that called the faithful to prayer. No doubt, Monty thought, the subject of the sermon would be the fire that had devastated the bus at *Tannenheim* castle the previous Wednesday. Prayers would be said for the rescue services despite the fact that the first eager fire engine had roared up the only metalled road so fast that it had skidded on the icy curve and overturned thus preventing other help vehicles from reaching the scene. Prayers would be offered for the perpetrators, who knew not what they had done, and for all those men, women and children who were trying to make a new life in Germany. Special prayers would go up asking God to help the three refugees who were still lying in intensive care, suffering from severe burns and hanging on somewhere between life and death.

The church bells also rang time on the gossip by Monty's front gate. Those standard English markers of "I've had enough of this conversation and want to go home" had been evident for some time in Julian's body language and intonation patterns and by Ingrid's legs, restless and sidestepping on her sensible heels. But Herr Maier was not tuned in to these subtleties of English communication. Through the glass of the front door, Monty watched the ensuing dance routine unfold. While Herr Maier advanced, tango-fashion, shopping bags were lifted and hands were proffered to be taken and shaken with smiles and nods. Both Ingrid and Julian had turned their shoulders to their pursuer when Monty backed into the kitchen.

Now is the time, Monty. What are you going to do – accuse him straight out or dig it out of him?

Opening the fridge, he took out a bottle of *Sekt* and glanced towards the entrance door. Even allowing for the distortions of the door glass, Julian did not create a favourable first impression. Nobody would have dared to use the word "misshapen" to describe him - at least, not to Ingrid or Monty - but even Monty had to admit that Julian's body was somehow out of balance, that each individual part of it was ill at ease with the whole. The shoulders, for example, were thin and curved but his legs were powerful tree trunks. One paediatrician had suggested that Ingrid's experiences in East Berlin, especially the spell in prison, might have had delayed consequences which caused poor maternal nutrition during later pregnancy. She certainly had been underweight and anaemic during that period, but this was a subject that was rarely broached in the Brodnitz household.

Monty drummed his thigh with his fingers and watched the two shadows loom up from the driveway to darken the front door glass. Seeing no sign of the persistent Herr Maier, Monty pulled two champagne flutes from the cupboard, hesitated and then added another. No need to exclude Julian like a pariah; no need to punish him for being the victim of poor maternal nutrition.

There was a hollow rattling sound from the other side of the front door. Monty assumed Ingrid was fumbling in her handbag for the door key. He picked up the bottle of *Sekt,* wrapped a towel around its neck and held the bottle into his groin while he extracted the cork. The hissing pop coincided with the click of a key turning in the lock. Monty sidestepped into the hallway. With the glasses in one hand and the bottle in the other, he put a smile of welcome on his face and tried to ignore the heart palpitations.

It was the receptive and attentive look in Monty's eye that died first. Then the spark went and Monty's emotional balance went with it. He had underestimated Herr Maier's persistence. The man was standing at the gate, waving his clip board over his head and pointing at it with his free hand. Monty did not want to hear for which cause he was now collecting signatures but he felt sorry for the man. He probably wanted to discuss the fire at the castle and feel the strength of the community in these times of stress or uncertainty.

When the door eventually swung open and the shadows at the door beamed into the house Monty was unprepared and he stared at the door in the manner of a child whose last friend had just deserted him. Ingrid flew past, her pony tail swinging in time to the clip clop of her shoes. She made a comment about having to get out of "these ridiculous heels" and disappeared up the stairs. Monty was alone when Julian burst in, head forward, with his arms at his sides as though someone had tied the cuffs of his jacket to the belt of his trousers.

Now was crunch time.

7

Friday – evening

Julian swivelled round his father and stood with one foot on the bottom stair. A ripple of distaste passed across his face as if he had caught the odour of something rotting in the fridge. He half-turned towards the kitchen where Monty was now making a show of checking the pasta bake.

"Does mum know? Have you told her?"

Julian was wearing very low-slung jeans, a hooded top and a baseball cap. Monty noticed that his son had not shaved. There were a couple of days growth covering parts of his face and making Julian's skin look mangy.

Does he think he looks cool?

"No, I haven't told her yet."

Monty heard Ingrid running the shower upstairs. Julian was still standing by the bottom step and watching him while a smile pulled at the corners of his mouth. A supercilious smile Monty thought - a smile that said, "Life is all about disappointments and you haven't faced them."

"No guts, eh, dad?"

Monty bit his tongue while poking at the bake he had pulled from the oven. He wondered whether this was a normal stage in the development of father-son relationships - the insult put as a rhetorical question, the father irritated while pretending to be interested in something else. Perhaps that was what happened to fathers, their role coming to an end once their children were old enough to cross the road alone. What did an adult father-son relationship look like anyway? He pushed the pasta bake back into the oven and slammed the door on it.

"I don't know what to say to her," Monty said. "The news will hurt her."

Monty was not expecting the impossible and comparing his relationship with Julian to his relationship with his own father - Max Brodnitz. That would be too much to expect. Nothing could ever match that model of perfection even if a hiccough later emerged in the shape of Ashley Mead. But a hiccough was never worth fretting over, never worth darkening the life or reputation of Max Brodnitz, father and hero, and model that Monty could emulate. Ashley Mead, like any hiccough, was not worth a moment's thought. Apart from his father, Monty had no precedent he could call on for help and no experience in life that could help him understand what was happening between him and Julian.

"I bet you don't know what to say, dad, do you?"

A thump from upstairs was followed by the hum of the hair dryer. He guessed Ingrid wanted to look her best for her only son. And ever since Ingrid had mentioned that Julian would be home for dinner on Friday night, Monty had been preparing himself in his way and working on his attitude. All his efforts had come to nothing.

"There is no need for her to know."

Julian laughed.

"Of course, there isn't. You would say that, wouldn't you?"

A part of him wanted to slap his son's face. Another part wanted to protect him - this boy who, in those very early years, liked to be a joker, to dress in strange clothes and walk in different ways. Julian had lots of friends at primary school and he wanted to be a helicopter pilot. Father and son had enjoyed such long cuddles. Those hugs with his child were tight and protective, but they gradually loosened as Monty went back to his work and, with a quick brush of hands, Julian ran off - the closeness gone in an instant. Even at the time he knew that one day the bodily parting would be permanent. Standing in the kitchen now and listening to his son, observing his what-do-I-care attitude, that warmth and contact were forgotten. In the grand scheme of things, it all seemed so meaningless.

"I wanted to speak to you first," Monty said.

"What do you expect from me?"

Monty was not expecting anything from his son. He was certainly not expecting a return to those days of cuddles. The last weekend Julian had been at home, he had spent most of his time in his room, his music even forbidding those distant shouts inviting him down for supper. When he did emerge, it was only to head for the front door and a quick exit.

"You reap what you sew, dad, didn't you know?"

Monty bit his lip and remained silent but he had often tormented himself with memories of his disappointing parenting skills. He wondered whether he would have been a more understanding and accepting father if his son had owned broader shoulders and a better-balanced physique. In these times of doubt, Monty convinced himself that had Julian been pretty he would have taken more care of him when securing him to the supermarket trolley and he would have kept toddler Julian in closer proximity to him when in a busy street. What these negative thoughts boiled down to, Monty convinced himself, was genetic legacy. Had Julian been a pretty and athletic child promising pretty and athletic children then Monty might have been a more attentive and loving father. As it stood, Monty thought, he had given his out-of-balance son so much space that he had slowly lost him in the city streets and the university where he had developed the out-of-balance mind he had witnessed at the castle.

"I do take some responsibility," he said.

"Some? Whose responsibility is it then, father? Don't you know how disappointed I am?"

"Disappointed?"

"I expected more from you."

Oh, I know about disappointments.

Monty believed that, with regard to Julian, disappointments were emotions he had learned to hide – one smile at a time. There was the polite smile when Julian's teacher reported that the boy was no good at the sports at which Monty had excelled. There was the embarrassed smile that hid Monty's disappointment while explaining to Julian that a poor head for heights did not make him a bad person. And there was the smile that Monty planted on his face when Julian showed no inclination to read the books Monty had read as a child. However, both father and son smiled with relief when the two of them shared an appreciation of the *Star Wars* series, which Monty likened to Greek and Roman myths in general and to Homer and Virgil in particular.

With disappointments came another emotion. His nights were spattered with guilt dreams in which the toddler Julian spent hours creating birthday cards for his father only to have paternal anger thrown back in his face because the colouring-in was somehow imperfect.

Perhaps Julian was aware of this and now hated the sight of this older man with greying hair and toneless age-freckled skin. He was probably an embarrassment, someone to make jokes about with his cronies at the university.

Monty opened the oven door, ducked as the hot air rushed over him and lifted the pasta bake from the oven. He was intending to throw out a casual comment but the tone of his voice rose with the temperature burning through the oven glove and into his fingers. His comment, "Perhaps we should not expect so much" ended on a strangled cry and was punctuated by a loud thump as the bowl landed hard on the sideboard. There was a sound of shuffling feet from the stairwell.

"I have a right to expect my dad to act his age."

Monty shook his hand and blew on his fingers before rushing to the sink and holding them under the cold water – just for a precaution. What a ridiculous comment Julian had made. It was flippant, too.

"What do you mean by that?" Monty said.

He congratulated himself. He had managed to keep his voice free of emotion and his tone down but his heart was fluttering wildly in his neck.

"Nothing."

This word - neither a statement nor a question - was a punctuation mark signalling the nothing-more-to-say-at-this-stage full-stop at the end of a paragraph. And then the sound of Julian, his footsteps making for the front door.

"I'm off out, OK. Don't wait up. You can have my share of the pasta, yeah?"

Monty lifted his fingers from the table and waggled his fingers. It was a gesture of what? If it were a gesture of farewell, he had not even looked up to see whether Julian had received it. Monty had not even bothered to lift his wrist from the table. His languid gesture merely said: if you hurt me, I will hurt you - tit for tat, an eye for an eye. What sort of behaviour was that from a 63-year-old? He was being pathetic.

Julian pulled open the front door, hesitated and turned around.

"How are you getting on with mum, dad?"

Monty stared at his son, shook his head and fumbled for something to say.

"Yes, dad, we need to talk," Julian said. "How long ago was it now? And the restaurant was Italian, wasn't it? And it wasn't mum you were with was it, dad?"

Monty gaped. His skin erupted in goose bumps as his mind shifted. A brief sense of panic pulled at his bowels before it all slotted into place. Julian thought his father was having an affair.

Monty knew many men of his age who had betrayed that all-important marital trust by having affairs with younger women. He was different. Monty had never thought of himself as a philanderer. He never saw himself as charming and a good listener. Not so long ago, however, someone in his office had told him that he was attentive and charming. In addition, he apparently looked people in the eye, took them seriously and made a woman feel that he wanted her company. What was more, he never looked over shoulders to see if someone more interesting was coming his way.

"You've lost me completely," Monty said.

"You're a lost soul, dad."

The speaker of these compliments was Daniela a 40-year-old new recruit in the accounting department of his office in the city. Business had been booming for some time and a new hand was needed. Daniela was the daughter of an Italian immigrant and she had been born and brought up in Germany. It seemed she was fond of older men and did not hesitate to let Monty know this. Monty saw now that Daniela was simply offering him an exchange of favours, a leg over for a leg up the company ladder.

"You are making a terrible mistake."

"That's what they all say, dad."

Initially, Monty was convinced that Daniela was looking for a kind of substitute father and was tempted to tell her to sort out her relationship with her parents. But, on second thoughts, and for a short time, Monty had seriously considered her offer. He was sixty-three and Daniela made him see the awful truth that there was no sex after life. He realised that he might not be able to perform to Daniela's expectations and the picture of a flaccid penis curled up and unresponsive in a bed of white pubic hair revolted and shamed him. Nonetheless, he owed it to himself to have a go. Along with these fears, there was his health to think of, but he managed to convince himself that he deserved one last fling before the grim reaper arrived to take him.

"There's nothing to say."

"Don't you think you should introduce me, dad?"

He and Daniela went out for lunch twice. The first time she had fumbled for his hand and stared dreamily into his eyes while they ate their *spaghetti alle vongole* in the small Italian restaurant which, Monty had lied, was well-known for its pasta. Actually, he had never been there but it was a safe distance from his office, near the university campus, and nobody would see them. The prospect of a second meal prompted Monty to have second thoughts. It was the very idea of all the underhand conspiracy that he could not tolerate: the lies, the excuses and the hiding. Worst of all, betrayal was something Ingrid would not suffer again. Betrayal was also something he did not approve of so he invited Daniela out once more and told her that they had better stop seeing each other in private. A hard look replaced the dreams in Daniela's eyes and her fumbling hand remained forever in the pockets of her designer jeans. He now kept away from her in the office but he had heard that Daniela was making quite an impact with the technicians recycling old models in the backroom.

"We need to talk about this relationship, father. But I tell you now I will not have it."

Further goose bumps, another mind shift, Julian's point of view.

He saw me fall from my pedestal. His idea of family is destroyed, his identity damaged. No wonder the drinking, the drugs. No wonder the Vaterlaendische Front.

"By the way," Julian said, "we just heard. One of the refugees died. Didn't you know?"

The door slammed shut. Julian was gone. Monty stared at the door. He heard a sort of strangled cough or cry, looked around as if there was someone else in the room and then raised his hand to his mouth in order to smother the sound that was coming from it.

8

Friday – evening

W e'd better start thinking of presents for Julian," Ingrid said. "Do you know what he'd like for Christmas?"

Monty looked up from his empty plate and at the extent of his failure rising over him. There was no going back to take a second shot at parenting and to repair the damage. Apart from alcohol and drugs, he had no idea what Julian actually liked. What was his favourite film? What music did he listen to? What sports did he like? Now he came to think of it, his ignorance was not confined to Julian's likes and dislikes. How tall was he? What had he done in his life that he was proud of? Did he have a nickname amongst university colleagues? Did he have a special friend?

"Maybe I can find something in my shop," he said.

"Monty, we need a plan. He is your son. You know him."

Monty grunted a non-committal response.

Not any more, I don't.

He had telephoned Julian's tutor the previous day. He

hardly recognised his son in the tutor's irritable hatchet job. Until very recently, Monty thought that because he had witnessed his child's birth, his first teeth, his first tentative steps, his first words, that he knew him. He shook his head.

He's a stranger to you, Monty.

The first pin to topple was Julian's intelligence. The tutor was not impressed by it. He told Monty that Julian was not doing too well. He had been skipping lectures and his performance was not up to scratch.

"His grades for the half-term tests were abysmal, Herr Brodnitz."

"Well," said Ingrid, "if you can't think of anything better than a piece of lost property, perhaps we should give him some money to spend on something he likes."

Like drugs?

The second pin to go was Julian's ability to distinguish between good and bad. Not a good score here.

"He's in with a bad crowd, Herr Brodnitz - smoking marijuana and drinking too much."

Monty had dismissed the tutor's allusion to homosexuality as spite. If Julian needed money, he needed only to ask for it. The notion that Julian would "buy" the pot, the smokes and beer from an older man in return for sexual favours was, simply, unacceptable and Monty threw the idea out and switched off the light on it.

"Does he have a girlfriend?" Ingrid asked.

"I think not," said Monty.

The tutor had also mentioned that Julian was being bullied in some way.

"Some of these bullies have thrown his books in the toilet and stolen his bag, Herr Brodnitz."

"They say it's going to be a warm Christmas," Ingrid said.

Her comment snapped Monty back to himself, to this

fishbowl room and to the mumble of the news broadcast on Channel 1. Actually, Monty was unable to comment on the weather at Christmas but after 22 years he knew Ingrid well enough to know that it was not the weather she wanted to talk about.

"Too warm for the time of year," she said.

He and Ingrid had met at the *Volkshochschule* in 1993. Monty had been so impressed by this countrywide adult education facility - VHS as it was commonly known - that on one of his periodic self-improvement trips he decided to enrol on an advanced German language and literature course and Ingrid was his teacher.

"Must be global warming," she said.

In later years, Monty liked to say that he had been impressed and inspired by his teacher's knowledge and dedication to her job. He rarely mentioned the long legs and the flaxen hair pulled back from the face into a long pony tail. He never acknowledged, not even to himself, that she reminded him of those ethereal photographs of his paternal grandmother Ida Brodnitz. Nonetheless, he was so taken by his teacher that, at the end of the course, he had decided to give her a gift and presented her with an item that had lain lost on a shelf in his offices in the city for several years - an author-signed copy of a Heinrich Boell novel entitled *The Bread of Our Early Years.*

"It really is time to do something about it, don't you think, Monty?"

This apparent reinforcement of her belief that those who came to live in Germany, either permanently or temporarily, should speak the language well enough to grapple with the German classics, clearly impressed her enough to accept his dinner invitation and the rest, as Monty was prone to say, was history. The previous year, she had been made Director of all language courses at the local VHS headquarters. She now had a platform upon which to develop her more radical ideas.

"Monty – what are you going to do about it?"

Monty always thought, although he never said it, that the spell in prison had left Ingrid with a flexible approach to life and the ability to adapt to circumstances. Monty found further evidence of this when Ingrid, much to her credit, realised that the current influx of refugees made Johann Wolfgang Von Goethe and Thomas Mann temporarily redundant. Grappling with *The Magic Mountain* or quoting from Goethe's *Der Erlkoenig* would be of little use to a young Syrian refugee anxious to buy food in the supermarket for his family, stamps at the post-office or to explain symptoms in the doctor's studio. They needed something other than, "Who rides so late through the wind and night? It's a father with his child so light."

"Monty...?"

This ability she had, to get to the heart of a topic, was usually introduced by a burst of silent activity around the house until Monty, not one to tolerate silence very well, would ask her what the problem was. At other times, her insights would be prefaced by a topic like the weather. They both knew the topic was a preamble but it gave Ingrid the time to get used to whatever was forming in her head. She might also be assessing his mood or state of mind in order to evaluate conditions and his ability to receive. They had been together long enough to acknowledge that a role-play was being acted out and it was usually played to Ingrid's rules - but not always.

"Where are you Monty?"

Monty also had his style of communication: typically British he thought, full of oblique references and implicit messages.

"Sorry, dear, but I've been waiting to tell you about what I've just been reading, about a kid in America.

He'd been failing and bullied at school."

"I see," Ingrid said pointing her fork in the direction of the television screen.

"Merkel will pay for her policies," she said. "Mark my words."

The volume control had been set, as it always was on Friday evening, by Ingrid. Thirty per cent capacity meant the TV could be heard but it was low enough to ignore if one wished to comment. Monty was not in the mood for commentary. He had to grab the moment, strike while the iron was hot and tell her before he could change his mind.

"The kid's response was horrifying," he said.

Ingrid was in her favourite reclining chair. Barefoot and with ankles crossed, her legs were stretched in front of her, and her pony tail was resting on her breasts. If her position was classic, there was something hunched about her shoulders which suggested she was tense. If he told her the truth, the whole truth and nothing but the truth she would want to know how he came by the information in the first place. For all her adaptability and intelligence, a person with her family background would hardly look kindly on her husband rifling through her child's belongings or spying on his movements. Monty braced himself.

"One day he took his father's long-barrelled 22-calibre revolver and 40 bullets to his high school in his school bag. He opened fire in the school toilets and then in the school quad. He killed two fellow students and wounded thirteen others."

Monty watched Ingrid's profile for any effect his words might have had.

"They need to change their gun laws," Ingrid said to the television set.

"But why would anyone do such a thing?" Monty said.

Her apparent refusal to engage with his story about an unknown child in the US filled Monty with something akin to despair. In a tone that was almost accusing he added:

"Suppose Julian did something like that. What would you say?"

"Julian would never do something like that."

"No, but suppose he did. What would you say?"

Monty waited - his heartbeat rising and fluttering in his neck. At the sight of her unresponsive shoulder, Monty was fearful that he would never be able to tell her unless he gave it to her directly - right between the eyes.

"I would say 'have faith,' Monty."

"Julian told me that one of the refugees died," he said.

"Well, actually..."

Ingrid fumbled for the remote and pointed it. The volume pins stretched across the screen from 30% to 49% exactly.

"The attack took place on Wednesday evening," the newscaster said. "Officials say that extremists are believed to have targeted the bus. One victim has since died from burns or the effects of inhaling smoke. Two other people are said to be critical. Police and forensic investigators are still working at the scene. One eyewitness told reporters that firemen were slow to arrive due to the weather conditions. A local shopkeeper in *Tannenheim* is reported as saying that said he saw several men fleeing from the scene on motorbikes. German cities and towns have been rocked by a series of attacks on refugees carried out by suspected right-wing extremists. So far this year there have been 222 violent attacks on refugee hostels by extremists. Each of the attacks either resulted in injuries or was of an intensity that they could have done so. Almost no cases have been resolved."

Ingrid lifted the remote and the volume pins reduced sound to 30%. Monty was shifting uncomfortably.

"But suppose he did do something like that, wouldn't it be..."

"They may have misunderstood," Ingrid said. "It is not a question of extremists. It is a question of fear. And you can understand, can't you, Monty? Helping people in need is one thing. Integrating a million people? That needs a lot of thought and brings a lot of fear."

His heart was pounding far too hard and fast. He expected to feel another irregular beat or flutter at any moment - an accompaniment to his indecision, his fear and his age. What was more, the school prefect was marching down the corridor and mouthing hugely.

"You're a coward and a baby, Brodnitz. Away with the fear and out with the truth, boy. Be man enough to suffer the consequences."

Monty braced himself again.

"I want to tell you something about..."

Ingrid turned sideways, found Monty's eyes with hers and silenced him with a smile.

"There is the fear of the ordinary citizen worried about terrorists," she said. "These ordinary people are worried for their children and grandchildren. The so-called extremists see themselves as patriots defending their homeland against a horde of refugees who don't want to learn about us, our language or our culture. Fear makes ordinary people do terrible things and support terrible acts."

Fear can also paralyse, Monty thought. He only had to look at himself in the mirror to see that. He had seen or heard the word "fear" a lot recently. Two days previously he had seen the word while searching his son's room. There were innumerable postings on the Facebook homepage of the *Vaterlaendische Front*. Most of them dealt with refugees, with fear and angst.

"I am afraid. I am afraid. I am afraid," wrote one lady from Frankfurt.

"We need to be afraid. The third world war has started without a shot being fired. In 70 years, people will be sitting in history lessons wondering how it happened."

"Wednesday is VF day - 18.30 - Schloss *Tannenheim*. Don't be afraid. Show your face and each person bring ten others with you."

Monty remembered - hearing his own disturbed breathing again while he scrolled down Julian's favourites, hearing the click of the mouse as he unlocked his own despicable behaviour and read his son's private emails.

"I'll be there and I look forward to it," Julian had written in response to the *Vaterlaendische Front's* leader, the *Sturmbannfuehrer*. "I do it for love of our homeland, for love of the truth and what is right. VF rocks! The EU, useless politicians, and mass immigration will walk over the grave of our wealth, our culture and the German people. How long can we let this go on?"

Monty stirred himself.

"I have been talking to Julian's tutor," he said.

Ingrid glanced up. There was a moment's silence.

"Why didn't you tell me?"

Monty was in no mood for the confrontation her tone seemed to demand. He looked across at her, her stiff face gradually softening into his silence and Monty shook his head - his final effort to tell her about Julian lacking punch and fizzling out.

"There's nothing much to tell."

She studied him, her eyes squeezed together as though she was looking at something a long way away.

"You must have faith, Monty. You know Julian better than you think you do."

Monty felt punctured, wanted to cover his face in his hands and hide his eyes from the unacceptable. He was simply inadequate both as a husband and a father.

"Why don't you go and stretch your legs, dear. You are as pale as a sheet, jittery and making me feel uncomfortable. But don't be long."

Monty nodded. "Stretching his legs" as Ingrid had put it, meant "you should go out for a Schnapps in the local bar" and they both knew it. He pushed himself out of his chair, his married life and his own dismal failure to put his wife in the picture.

"Monty?" Ingrid cried out as he laid his hand on the door handle.

Monty froze.

"I have something to say to you when you get back," Ingrid said. "It's very important and you must prepare yourself for what I have to say. Please Monty. I can't put it off any longer."

Monty pulled his coat round him, hurried out into the cold air and closed the door behind him. The smell of fire hung over the town - a sort of sooty dampness. He tried to find other adjectives to describe the smell. The words "burnt plasticky" sounded good and so did "sweet gunpowdery," "charring fleshery" and "concrete dustery" but whichever expression he used the smell was the same and so were the feelings of cowardice and guilt they evoked.

A few seconds later he was on the corner and looking up the main street towards the care home and the hill behind it that rose up to the castle. It seemed to Monty that the world was out of focus. True, the bank was where it always was and the supermarket was lit up in the headlights of arriving or departing cars, but he felt as if he had fallen asleep and, like Rip Van Winkle, had woken up in a world that was recognisable but somehow different. Perhaps something inside him had shifted or,

God help him, it was the start of dementia.

The main street was full of dark-skinned young men silently perusing their mobile devices. Homeless and lost in a foreign country, they were curved over their phones or holding them on their knees in the manner of a new parent holding a baby. He sympathised with them. He too felt somehow lost to the world. The restless energy that had pushed him forward, the urge to find his son and to ask him about himself and to undo his own failure, suddenly deserted him completely. He leaned against a tree and felt a bead of sweat forming on his brow and a flutter in his neck. The sweat rolled down his temple, hung there while he considered Ingrid's request. Prepare yourself, she had said. His mind was spinning. Perhaps Ingrid had found out that he had been searching Julian's room. Perhaps Julian had told her that he had been having an affair with a woman at work. He thought he knew her well enough to guess what she was going to do. Once she had made up her mind, there was no changing it.

Maybe she is going to leave you, Monty.

9

Friday – late evening

He considered life without her until the bead of sweat took off from his temple, accelerated down his cheek and dropped to his shoe. Monty watched it glittering in the lamplight before pushing himself away from the tree. A little breathless, Monty headed off in the direction of the care home at the top of the high street. Dragging his feet, he managed to trip over a loose paving stone, lost his balance and nearly fell to the ground.

For God's sake, Monty, get a grip. You're just joining your son for a drink. There's nothing to feel bad about.

But he avoided the light of the street lamps and concealed himself by walking between the trees that lined the street. The trees gave him something to relate to, an area where he was inconspicuous but connected. To hell with everyone and what they thought, he would stay under the cover of the trees until he reached the neon lights of Bar Villa Italia.

Starting out from one tree to the next Monty felt his

heart thump again. There was no point denying that he was breathless. It had to be the cold air that was detrimental to his lungs although the cold was at odds with the film of sweat on his brow. No doubt it was his behaviour that he found as difficult to stomach as Ingrid did. It was provoking an internal conflict that raised his body temperature.

He took a deep breath and blew out his cheeks. *You could hardly blame her if she left you, could you, Monty?* He pursed his lips and exhaled through them. Shaking his head, he reminded himself that he, too, had a dislike of the underhand and those who skulked in the shadows. Monty clung on to the next tree almost as if it were his lifeline. His underhand behaviour was different. Rifling through Julian's possessions was a sign of his love. He had wanted to protect his son, to find something in Julian's room that would force him to disbelieve his own eyes. His spying was good spying and not to be confused with the bad spying of Ingrid's parents and brother in East Germany in the eighties. Monty shook his head again. Ingrid was no fool.

Good spying, Monty? That is what they all said. Accept it, man. You have been outed. You are both a sneak and a philanderer and you are going to pay for it.

He was unsteady on his legs when he set off up the street again, drifting between the trees, falling from one piece of cover to another where he could cling on and feel safe. It was a roar of laughter and a babble of voices that told him he was outside the Bar Villa Italia. Wiping at his brow, Monty scanned the interior of the bar until Julian appeared in his line of sight. He was standing amongst a group of other men whose youth and gaiety distinguished them from the others. Someone put a hand on Julian's arm and whispered in his ear. Julian exhaled as if releasing tension. He looked relaxed and happy, a man amongst other men enjoying a beer on a Friday night. Monty drifted along with this idea for a while but tumbling to the front of his mind, unstoppable and relentless, came the realisation that this was the post-demonstration party "To decorate the heroes. To celebrate a victory for Germany," the *Sturmbannfuehrer* had written in his email.

Once the truth was out, memories of other mails and Facebook posts he had read on Julian's computer came with it.

"The finest of goose flesh. Thank you, *Tannenheim*," one Facebook poster had written. "It is a good feeling to stand with you and with our culture, our values. I come from Dresden - there and back 1000 km. And so what? Next week - Berlin!!"

"Thousands of VF patriots were there despite the icy weather."

And now some of them were here to celebrate the post-mortem. Feeling the bile rising into his throat, Monty swallowed hard to stop himself from retching. He felt his mind shift again and almost walked straight into a group of men smoking under an awning by the entrance. They began muttering something in concerned tones. Maybe they thought the old man wiping sweat away from his brow and gagging was about to have a stroke or a heart attack. They were conversing in Polish and Monty felt the need to connect with them and tell them that when he was a child his greatest friend, Paul, had been the son of a Polish immigrant who had fled to England in 1940. One of the defining episodes of Monty's life came from his childhood friendship with Paul. This particular episode was magnificent, a monument to Englishness, to good behaviour and something he referred to when he needed to find himself, to connect with right and wrong.

Monty smiled at the Poles and, muttering an apology in their direction, he turned away from them, bowed his head to the wind and set off back down the street towards his house. He found he was still walking from shadow to shadow - hiding when he no longer had a need to hide. He hardly noticed the wind at first but it was flushing out the dead leaves and paper from the gutter and blowing them into the air. He tried to focus on the leaves and avoid the questions that turned in his head and pulled at his stomach.

Stretch my legs?

He shook his head and screwed up his eyes.

Prepare myself?

Monty quickened his pace.

For what? My comeuppance?

He was almost running when a heart-flutter brought him to a halt. He leaned against a tree for support and bent over at the waist in order to regain his breath. It was a while before Monty realised that the nearest street lamp had gone out and he was standing in complete darkness. Fortunately, he knew where he was. During the day, this part of the street was always a shady place lined on one side with an overgrown building plot and, on his side, with gnarled trees that blocked out any natural light from above. If he turned, he would see the bright lights of the care home and the Villa Italia. Instead, Monty almost smiled into the lonely stretch of darkness that led in front of him to his street and his house.

At first, he thought he heard the trees rustling in the breeze. But the rustling increased until Monty believed he was detecting - not the movement of branches - but whispering voices. The sounds were coming from the other side of the tree where a bench had been erected. He raised his head. A hoarse voice growled out words and punctuated them with a persistent cough.

"Nobody really listened to me... I did my best to...to warn them...but it wasn't one of us..."

"Us?"

"The townsfolk - you and me - us."

"Mizzi says it must be foreigners. Germans don't do that sort of thing."

"The petrol bombing?"

The petrol... It was too much."

"Maybe the man lost control."

"Lost control? He filled a bottle, stuffed old rags in the neck, brought it up to the castle, lit the rag and threw it. Sounds like he knew exactly what he was doing."

"It might have been an accident."

"Premeditated."

"Could be."

"Mizzi thinks it was a prank that got out of hand."

"Maybe."

"Our man could be a pyromaniac?"

"Our man?"

A strong gust of wind blew the response away and the two men rose as one and stepped up the street towards the Bar Italia.

"Absolutely," Herr Maier said. "Mizzi says accidents like that can happen."

As their words receded again to a rustle in the air, Monty thought that what he had seen at the castle could well have been a prank that got out of control. Equally, he could be grasping at straws. The compulsion to start fires might have been an affliction Julian had inherited from his father. Monty's early escapade with Paul suggested this might be the case.

Monty cast his mind back and tried to relive the whole childhood experience in a series of time slices and visual images. He found that each brought with it its own emotional response - guilt and fear, and sadness that Paul was long since dead. The first picture was the hedge. It flanked Paul's garden in Long Ditton village and there was a row of three garages behind it. Whose idea it had been to light a fire in one of the garages was lost to him but the next image was of him and Paul with some greasy rags, a tin of liquid from Paul's garden shed and a box of matches from the kitchen.

In later years, both individuals would discuss this episode over a beer and it emerged that both had different memories of the same event. Paul said that he remembered his friend, almost possessed by the devil, taking the lead, moving them forward. Monty merely recalled his friend trying to put the fire out with the liquid from the petrol tin. Both shuddered at the memory of the ensuing fireball that could have killed them. Neither had a good explanation as to why they were not killed or severely burned. But the uncomfortable truth was that the fire got out of control and all three garages went up in smoke. The fire brigade was called and the whole area was sealed off.

The local Long Ditton police took little time finding convenient culprits. The Cole children - Nigel and Steffi - were the local baddies. Their clothes were dirty, their shoes had holes in them and the two children stank. Their father, the local coal merchant, was reputed to be a bad man, who abused his children in ways that were never actually spelled out. Permanently streaked with coal dust, Mr Cole was often to be seen tramping through the village towards the local pub - the George and Dragon - where he would take an extended lunch. Apparently, the Cole children were seen in the vicinity of the fire. This was hardly surprising given that they spent all the daylight hours playing in the streets until their father came home. Of course, they were guilty. What was more, Nigel had a penknife attached to his belt and someone said that Steffi had been playing with what looked like matches.

Monty thought that Steffi's affliction made her a target. He recalled seeing her for the first time. She had been hobbling around the village in her callipers and trying to sell the flowers she had picked from fields nearby. In retrospect, Monty realised Steffi was lucky. Many victims of Polio were unable to move except with great hardship using big wooden crutches. Their legs were encased from top to bottom in a complex arrangement of steel bars and leather straps that tightly held their withered limbs straight. Steffi had something much simpler on her legs, something which came up to just below the left knee. She seemed able to get about a bit more easily but still she was the object of stares and curiosity. She might just as well have been punished by God himself for some sin she or her family had committed.

At the time, Monty never asked himself what had happened to her or what it was like to be like her. He did not ask himself how she could play if she could not run about. She must have been in the vicinity of the fire and, unable to run away, she got caught and took the blame.

Immediately after the fire, Monty had been delighted that he had got away with it. It was not long before uncomfortable feelings began to keep him awake at night. At Long Ditton Primary School his teachers complained that he was withdrawn, and in the playground, he got into fights with older kids. The ensuing beatings seemed somehow well deserved. Two weeks after the fire, he surprised himself by getting off the bus and, instead of going to school, he walked to the police station and confessed.

"It was me. I burned the garages down," he announced to a rather surprised policeman. When asked why he had not owned up sooner, Monty simply burst into tears. The relief at not having to carry that guilt about was something he never forgot. His father had been understanding about the whole incident and even praised Monty for displaying such moral courage.

Reaching the corner of his street, Monty came to an abrupt halt.

Moral courage, Monty? You did not give a fig about Nigel and Steffi Cole. Your confession was for you and you alone. Selfishness guided your actions then as it guides them now.

His confession might have helped the young Monty but there was no evidence that it had helped Steffi and Nigel. Those poor kids were probably doomed from the day of their birth. Monty had never sought confirmation but hearsay had it that by the time she reached 15 years of age, Steffi was pregnant and living in a run-down council estate on the edge of town. Nigel had been in and out of borstal several times and probably ended up in prison. So, what had been the point of Monty doing the right thing? Perhaps he should have allowed them to take responsibility for the fire, and who knows? Maybe Nigel and Steffi would have learned a lesson and their lives might have been different.

Monty was lighter of foot when he strolled along the pavement towards his house. The thought that deliverance might come through confessing everything to his wife even prompted him to look around him. He noticed that the lights in the Villa Rosa suggested that Peter Lutz was at home. He even noted that the weather had changed since the night of the attack. It was now unseasonably warm and the odd spot of thick rain struck his hand or temples but he loosened his coat and filled his lungs with fresh, clean air. In a burst of positive energy, he thought that, with any luck, the wind would blow away the sickening smell of burning. With any luck, Ingrid would be sympathetic and forgive him. With any luck, she would decide to stay.

When he turned into his driveway, the air was alive with bits of tree blowing across the road or else they were sucked upwards, twirling and turning to disappear in the darkness. He fumbled for his key. His hand was firm as he tried to fit the key in the lock. His heart was beating regularly as he pushed at the door and tiptoed into a house already settling into the night. Easing the door shut, Monty stood in the entrance hall, listening. The hall was filled with rustlings and creaks and a vague smell of disinfectant. He crept into the sitting-room and felt more secure. The gentle pitter-patter of rain on the windows connected him to the world outside and his mood lifted. He stepped towards the drinks table and scanned the bottles and decanters for several seconds before removing a glass stopper and pouring himself a whisky.

A reflection materialised in the huge windows. It was Ingrid and she was standing squarely in the doorway. Initially, he thought she had come to wish him a good night but she was fully clothed. If Monty had not known that his wife lived in a cry-proof state, he might have thought that she had been weeping but the tears were an illusion conjured up by the water streaming on her reflected window-image.

Monty shook his head, removed the metal stopper again and poured out another whisky.

"Drink?"

Now was the time, the time to do the right thing, come clean and apologise. He held out the drink, stood like a traffic policeman until he heard her shuffle towards him. He span around. His mouth was already open and ready to enunciate the words "I must tell you about Julian and I have a confession." He was too late. Ingrid spoke into his space:

"I can't go on like this," she said.

Ingrid removed the drink from Monty's outstretched hand and the way she looked at him silenced him before he could utter a word more. He breathed out through his nose while she held his gaze.

"I have come to a decision."

These words were spoken into the glass she had raised to her lips. Monty pulled away and sat down on the sofa. His moment had come and gone. The denial of truth that lay between them was exposed and he was going to pay the price. Monty ran a hand through his sweeping hair, his eyes darting from side to side while he searched for something useful to say. But he knew that once Ingrid had decided on a course of action, the plan was set in stone. It would need an earthquake to change her mind.

"I am leaving tomorrow," she said.

Monty stared through the window, through the tears of rain pouring down the glass. He saw the lawyer's office, the furniture removal van carrying his belongings to temporary housing. To one side of the van he saw his son, hands to head, asking, "Why?" Monty refocused on his own image reflected in the glass but somehow it was now distorted as though about to fall apart.

10

Friday – late evening

L eaving for Berlin," Ingrid said. "I'll take the early morning flight and be there by mid-morning. I already bought the ticket and I'd like you to drive me to the airport."

She paused, just long enough for Monty to raise any objections and then she nodded.

"Good. There's no question about it. I'm going to Berlin. I shall face my parents before they die, talk to them, tell them I forgive them. You see, don't you, Monty? What they did to me was not their fault? Monty? Speak to me. You look like you saw a ghost."

Monty looked up, his smile beaming out his joy at being with Ingrid and his relief that she wanted to be with him. He longed to sing it out, cast joy's light over the world and tell everyone that marital happiness was within their reach and waiting to be grasped. He said:

"Oh, what a good idea."

Ingrid cocked her head.

"Do you mean that, Monty or are you using your English sarcasm?"

She turned away from the drinks' table and lifted her drink to nose level, watched Monty over the brim of the glass before taking a sip that barely wetted her lips.

"Monty, please - this is no time for your silly English jokes. Some things should be treated with reverence."

Monty raised his arm to silence her and shook his head. Sarcasm was rarely used by Germans and seldom appreciated when and if they recognised it. It usually left them bewildered.

"Sarcasm? No, no," he said. "But I was wondering about the timing."

"The morning flight?"

Monty shook his head again.

"The timing of forgiveness. Isn't it a bit late?"

This was not really a question, but Ingrid answered it with a measure of calm patience.

"Children expect their parents to be perfect. Even when the children are adults, it's easy for them to forget that their mums and dads are human beings with all the strengths and weaknesses that go with it. The war, and what happened afterwards, was the decisive event in my parents' lives. It shaped their values and made them who they are. I never experienced such a catastrophe so what right do I have to condemn them?"

"That's no reason why you should have to pay the price for their suffering."

She held up her hand to silence him but Monty was not to be put off.

"They betrayed you and..."

"No, no..."

Avoiding Monty's eyes, Ingrid vigorously shook her head, her long pony tail flying.

"They didn't know what they were doing."

"But..."

"No 'buts,' Monty. It's never too late to forgive."

Ingrid turned her back on him and filled her glass

with water. Monty heard the glass stopper scraping the neck of the bottle and waited for her to swing round and face him. Memories of his own father, now dead and unpardoned, came and went with the light that was winking in the window of the Herr Maier's house on the other side of the street. The light appeared and disappeared with the swaying of the trees in the wind and the echo of Ingrid's word "forgive." Raindrops threw themselves against the window with a sound of pebbles.

Monty nodded his head, once, twice and then several times.

"OK," he said. "I can understand the need to forgive."

He looked up at her and smiled.

"Actually, it's an admirable thing to do."

But - why the suddenness? Ingrid's rejection of her parents has always been a part of the natural order of things, hasn't it, Monty?

"But out of the blue like this? What has happened to change you?" Monty said. "Why now?"

Monty looked expectantly at her back while awaiting her reply. His expectations dissolved in the long silence and the turn of his own thoughts. It occurred to Monty that, whichever way you looked at Ingrid, front or back, she did not look her age of fifty. From where he was sitting, her figure suggested a much younger woman despite the birth-hangover handles pushing through her pullover and the water-retention-puffiness in the skin of her hands and neck. Sexual attraction might have brought them together but it was not what kept them together and from falling apart. Monty believed their marital success was based on trust, and trust had developed as a by-product of being there for each other when it was not always convenient, of telling the truth when it might have been easier to lie and of keeping promises when they might have got away with breaking them.

Trust, Monty thought, had been aided and abetted by balance, their individual differences challenged and compensated for by the other. Many of these differences, Monty knew, had their origin in culture - differences in values mixed in with peculiarities of personality that could be interpreted in a dozen different ways. The differences in values might have been problematic but, on another of his regular self-improvement trips, he had taken a weekend course in Intercultural Communication at the university in the city. There he learned that having a personal opinion and expressing it was expected and valued in the UK and learning to defend these views without taking offence was also highly valued and appreciated. But Germany was not the UK. So many things here were still taboo and the tendency to identify personally with your views meant that an attack on views was an attack on the individual. At this time, he thought it prudent to remain laconic. Ingrid's relationship with her parents was as personal as it could get.

Monty watched her pony tail swinging from side to side like the pendulum of a grandfather clock. Maybe she had not heard his question about the timing of her forgiveness. Maybe she was away with her own thoughts and formulating questions of her own. Eventually, she said:

"Imagine what it must have been like for the refugees. Meeting people, hostile people mostly, for just a couple of hours, to see the worst in humanity and then move on. What sort of fear does that leave in you? What scars does that leave?"

"Which refugees do you mean? The ones attacked at the castle?"

Ingrid shrugged and then shook her head.

"The ones attacked two days ago? The ones who were forced out of the Sudetenland in 1945 and 1946? Unfortunately, it probably means any refugee, from any time and in any place."

"Would you care to elaborate?"

Monty looked up expecting Ingrid to reply. He saw, instead, that something was moving inside her - possibly a change of view - and that, Monty knew, was often problematic for Germans in general and for Ingrid in particular. When the new view was eventually formed, it was perfectly shaped and came with instructions for use and a guarantee of ten years. Monty envied her the degree of flexibility which she was displaying. He seemed to have mislaid his flexibility somewhere. He had become more detached, judgmental and, consequently, his own views had become more fixed than they had been 20 years previously.

"Elaborate? There's nothing left to say, Monty."

Nonetheless, he accepted that Ingrid did things differently and, he believed they were allies despite their differences. Received wisdom suggested that he was more daring, more adventurous and more intellectual and that Ingrid was cautious, conventional and less changeable in mood and ideas. But Monty was aware that circumstances could change without warning. Perhaps they were going through a circumstance change now. After all, she was the one who was about to do the daring and adventurous thing and travel to Berlin. Worse than that, his integrity and trustworthiness were under attack in the shape of his indecision, his lies and silences.

"Yes, I meant any refugee from any time in any place. Sad isn't it?"

Monty recognised Ingrid's conservative characteristics in her attitude to marriage, to her job at the VHS, and to many of her opinions and feelings.

Safety was in the status quo. Change was a necessary evil. Betrayal was unforgivable. Betrayal of her by her family to the authorities had, until recently it seemed, amounted to sin. He sometimes resented her black and white view of the world and he sometimes admired it. His own views were, he believed, typically British in that they were full of half-rights and half-wrongs and all the shades of doubt between.

"Doesn't say much about us, does it?" Monty said, almost to himself.

"Us?"

"Yes, us - the great European public."

They remained lost in their own thoughts, while the wind rose in intermittent moans, followed by noises that brought to Monty's mind the sound of sails flapping and cracking. The wind was whipping up the trees in the garden and they now threw themselves from side to side as if attempting to free themselves from a predator's grip.

"It's easy to blame your parents," Ingrid said. "It's easy to make them responsible. And all we have to do is point our finger at them and tell them what lousy parents they were. That makes us cowards, Monty. We make ourselves victims - poor little victims."

There was a howl from outside and the house seemed to shake as it was gripped in a rush of air. The windows and doors rattled to the sound of flapping sheets. Monty was about to check that he had closed the front door securely when she turned away from the table to face him.

"Well, I have had enough of being a victim. I can take responsibility and forgive them for what they did. We cannot change what happened or what my parents did but I can change how I react to it."

Monty crossed and then uncrossed his legs and leaned forward to rest his forearms on his knees. He let his head fall forward and a lock of his huge and sweeping hair fell with it. Brushing the hair back, he eyed his glass, watched the whisky ripple as it picked up a vibration running down his arm and into his fingertips. He stared, fascinated, while his mind worked backwards, retraced his life and stopped with his father Max. He shook his head while Ingrid walked past him and made towards the door, head high. Her eyes were set forward and her footsteps were measured and firm. She had made up her mind and that was an end to the matter. There was little point in discussing this decision further she would have said and Monty had to agree. At the door, Ingrid turned around.

"Tomorrow," she said, "when we are on the way to the airport, I am going to tell you a story about my father. Maybe this will help you understand my decision. Oh, and there is one other thing."

For a second or two, the force of Ingrid's tone obliged Monty to keep his silence. A recent convert, he thought, would not tolerate dissent. Furthermore "one other thing" usually meant something of huge importance. Ingrid said:

"How do you say '*Man kann einen alten Baum nicht verpflanzen*' in English?"

"You can't uproot an old tree? We say 'You can't teach an old dog new tricks'."

Ingrid nodded. She was gazing upwards and over Monty's head while she decided what to say next. She took a deep breath.

"*Scheiss*, Monty, total S*cheiss*. Stuff and nonsense. This idea has been put into our heads by teachers and parents and what happens? It becomes an excuse for being stagnant and inflexible."

"Oh..."

"You, Monty, must not allow the past to keep you a prisoner inside yourself."

"I don't think I understand..."

"Please listen, Monty. I have something else to say that can wait no longer."

She stared right into him and raised her index finger.

"When I come back, I want to see your problems with Julian sorted."

Monty opened his mouth to speak but she silenced him with the raised finger now wagging between her eyebrows. He had been preparing himself to tell her about Julian and about his own guilt but he had been pre-empted, finessed with finesse and, essentially, silenced by Ingrid's moving finger.

"Just do it, Monty," she said. "I don't care how and I don't want to hear about it. Just do it and then we can all move on."

"But..."

"No 'buts,' Monty and I promise you one thing."

Somewhere in the town an angry car horn was answered by shouts of abuse. Then came the thumping roar of motorcycle engines and the screech of tyres. A parade of motorbikes filed past the house, all noise and hair, German military helmets, and everything burly, bearded and threatening. Ingrid shook her head. She waited for the bikes to pass and said:

"I promise you now that I won't ask questions."

She nodded at Monty, turned and left the room. He remained on the sofa for a few seconds eyeing the drinks cabinet and contemplating another whisky. There was a voice from the stairwell.

"I have been thinking about the Christmas decorations. I've put them in the loft."

A shooting pain in his toe prompted Monty to shout:

"What have you done with the suitcase?"

There was no answer from Ingrid but there was a man's voice in his ear from behind.

"Why have I never heard about this problem before?"

It was Julian. Pale and frail, he was standing at the door - questions furrowing at his brow and about to be articulated.

11

Friday – night

"That depends on which problem you are referring to," Monty said, deciding to have a glass of whisky after all. Still with his back to Julian, he got up, stepped towards the drinks table and twisted the metal stopper from the neck of the decanter. It set up a sound not dissimilar to the warning call of monkeys and put Monty's teeth on edge. He splashed some whisky into the glass, replaced the stopper and flicked his head in his son's direction. Julian was a vague shape in his peripheral vision. At that moment, Monty wished he would stay that way. He doubted it. The boy was breathless, he had had a few drinks and his tone suggested he was ready for a confrontation. Nevertheless, Julian should not be talking to his father like that. Monty considered lecturing his son on good manners but, predicting the resulting tetchiness, the low-level bickering that might follow, he decided to keep quiet.

"I've been standing in the corridor for some time," Julian said. "I can tell you exactly what the problem is."

"And?"

"I told you earlier, father. I saw you with another woman. Who was she? I have a right to know. Who was she?"

This question did not require an answer concerning the name of a woman. It was accusatory and resentful and demanded an explanation. What was more, the choice of the word "father" seemed designed to be hurtful. For Monty, the word represented the male parent, someone who was responsible for the conception and birth of a baby. He would have liked to hear Julian use the word he had always used with his own father. The word was "dad." "Dad" was the man who supported the child by providing parental care, food, shelter and clothing but above everything a dad was the person who provided love. Being a father was something every man could do. Being a dad was special, required a huge effort and defined the long-term relationship between man and son.

"You surprise me," Monty said.

"Don't wriggle out of..."

"Can't a man and a woman have lunch together without being accused of having an affair? What year are you living in – 1916?"

Monty turned around, his gaze settling on the weak shoulders, the strands of hair falling from Julian's cap and tickling his neck. Although the hair was delicate and promised early loss, Monty wanted to think that Julian was not much more than an overstretched boy with an attitude problem. But the low-slung jeans and the baseball cap irritated him. Worse was the formal way in which Julian structured his words and thoughts. He sounded as if he were giving a prepared speech but, at the same time, it would not have been a surprise to hear Julian punctuating his speech with those equally irritating hand signals Monty had seen on rap videos.

"A while ago, father, I came to see you. I wanted you to read something I had written; a poem, actually, but I saw you with someone else."

Julian lowered his head and glanced towards the door through which his mother had gone. He whispered in a tone of incredulity:

"I saw you having a meal with a younger woman. Who was it, father?"

The whispered question now suggested an intimacy between the two of them that confused Monty further. He furrowed his brow in order to let Julian know he was thinking.

"How long ago did you say this happened?"

"Don't know. Some months ago, I would..."

"Some months? Why did you not come to me sooner?"

"It's not easy to bring up such a subject and accuse your father of having an affair."

"Really?"

"Really."

"You really didn't have the courage to confront me, did you? Let me ask you again - am I not permitted to have lunch with people of the opposite sex?"

"Not if you're having an affair."

Monty swallowed a laugh. The boy was serious.

"You know, don't you, father, an affair with another woman is betrayal – betrayal of mum, betrayal of me..."

"It sounds," Monty said, almost to himself, "like she is the new employee I took to lunch."

He smiled as he spoke, smiled in the same way that he used to smile at Julian when he was around twelve years old. Those were the good times, when Julian had been such a warm-hearted, kind and patient boy. On his way home from school he laughed and greeted everyone he met. In retrospect, Monty recalled that Julian had never actually stopped to speak to anyone, but other parents often commented how nice and friendly Julian was. What an insipid word "nice" was. With a grin of remembrance, Monty recalled Julian's modesty and his son's frequent comment that a smile could change people's lives. What a nice thing to say, Monty thought. How nice that Julian had helped to take those lives away the previous Wednesday. No amount of "nice" smiling would change anything there.

"New employee? Are you kidding? The way she was behaving? She was all over you, father. Come on, who was it? One more time, are you having an affair?"

Monty lifted his glass and tossed its contents into his mouth. Julian had started showing his true colours when he was around fifteen. The family were attending the funeral of one of Ingrid's colleagues, who had unexpectedly died in a car accident. After the service, Julian had asked him whether it was normal to feel superior to the dead. "You have survived," Julian said. "You have outlived the guy in that coffin. You have been anointed, marked as special and asked to live."

Now at twenty, he was showing the same cynicism, the same callousness. Worse still, he seemed to be projecting it onto his own father.

"An affair at my age?" Monty said. "Are you joking? I don't have the energy."

Perhaps, Monty thought, Julian's cynicism had developed alongside Monty's concerns about his son's sexuality, his smallness, his sullen moodiness. There seemed to be only disappointment left between them. It really was not supposed to be like that. Memories of children were supposed to be things to treasure, but Monty was simply unable to bring back the memory of a smile that would change the world.

"No, I am not joking," Julian said, "and no, you are not too old."

Or perhaps it was the fragility of the present that was

the problem and he was and had always been at fault. Monty had recently read an online article suggesting that older fathers were associated with autistic and schizophrenic children and boys and girls who failed at school. For so long, mothers - particularly older mothers - had taken responsibility for genetic disorders in their children. The article pointed out that since eggs were stored from birth and not made anew with each monthly reproductive cycle, they could develop genetic mutations. Fathers, on the other hand, constantly made sperm that was fresh and free from accumulated DNA damage. However, a genetic analysis in 2012 turned up something new. Apparently, mutations could occur in the sperm of older men. Monty now questioned whether he was responsible for Julian's problems: the drugs, his poor performance at the university, the fire, and the death.

Responsible or not, Monty was not going to let Julian get away with accusing him like that.

"How dare you say these things to me," he said.

Monty turned and poured himself another whisky.

Better be careful with the drink, Monty.

He poured less whisky and more water into his glass and made a show of replacing the metal stopper carefully, noiselessly. In the window, he was able to see the reflection of his son. His mouth was open and his fists clenched. Monty could almost feel his anger bursting forth and burning into his back in the manner of a science-fiction ray gun.

Go easy, Monty. At least he has had the courage to talk to you which is more than can be said for you with your father. You never did speak to him, did you? You never had the guts.

"You have evidence to back your claims, I suppose?" Monty said.

"I know what I saw."

"You know what you saw," Monty said to the ceiling. "If only it was that easy."

"It is that easy, father. That was no ordinary meal you were having."

No, and nor was your father's behaviour ordinary, was it, Monty? Where were your guts when you needed them? You had better show Julian the respect he deserves.

Monty made a show of correcting the position of the metal stopper. The stopper was so cold to the touch that Monty had a sudden vision, a mental glimpse of himself getting out of bed early one freezing January morning many years previously. He wanted to ensure the house would be warm enough for baby Julian when he woke up. Monty shook his head and swung round.

"First," he said, "I want to talk about last Wednesday."

"I said I know what I saw - so who was she, father?"

Julian took a couple of steps towards him but his moment and his initiative had passed. His eyes were already wandering around the room as though he was looking for answers to the questions he knew were coming.

"You were at the demonstration last Wednesday, weren't you? Please don't deny it."

Monty was careful to keep his tone neutral, non-judgemental.

"I saw you, you know?" Monty said, lifting his glass and holding it up in front of him as though about to make a toast. "Yes, I did, you know, white robes and all. K.K.K outfit wasn't it?"

He used the abbreviation to indicate that he was an insider, knew what he was talking about, although he knew little concerning the Klu Klux Klan except that it was the oldest organisation in the US bringing its message of hope and deliverance to White Christian

America.

Julian had gone quite pale. But Monty said nothing more. He watched his words force a shift in Julian's expression from shock to something resembling sorrow. Watching his son now, Monty was aware of a variety of thoughts and feelings that were competing for his attention. The first thought to come to him was how much he owed to his own father. Do not accuse. Do not judge. Just state the facts. These were dictums his father had lived by and Monty had adopted them and used them as his own. He was employing them now with his own son. How else could a man learn how to be a father other than by using his own as a role model? His father was almost 30 years dead now but Monty still worshipped the ground he had walked on – quite literally. Five years previously his neighbour, Peter Lutz, had sold off the chunk of land on which Monty's own house now stood. This meant that the land under Monty's feet had belonged to his forebears. It was land on which his father would have walked, played and conversed.

The second thought that came to him was that not everything had been plain sailing with his father. Even now he found it difficult and painful to reconcile the reality of the man with the hero Monty had created for himself.

Being Jewish, the hero fled Germany in May 1939 after spending 6 months in Dachau concentration camp. During his confinement, Max had seen men dropping dead from exhaustion, from violence and neglect. Even after his release from Dachau, Max knew that, sooner or later, the Nazis would come back for him. He implored his parents and other family members to come with him to England but they stayed and Max went. "If it hadn't been for Britain, I would have died along with my family," Max often said. "There would be no you,

Monty, and Max Brodnitz would simply be a name engraved on a sixth *Stolperstein* outside the gates of a house in *Tannenheim*."

"Just to be clear," Monty said to his son, "I saw you. I saw what you did. I think you had better tell me about it. Then, we can decide what to do next."

He watched Julian's gaze slide away. The boy removed his cap and held it with both hands against his stomach. His face was fully exposed to the light and Monty noticed the purple lines under his eyes. He looked tired, or perhaps, Monty thought, the lines were the result of taking drugs. His own father would surely have disapproved of taking mind-changing substances. Monty certainly disapproved and not only because they were against the code of conduct instilled in him by his old school.

When he was sixteen, Monty had taken a summer job in the cafeteria at Hampton Court Palace. It was rumoured that the young man on the washing-up machine, Stuart, was a heroin addict. Monty kept his distance from Stuart but kept an eye on his movements. Monty soon noticed that the washing-machine would often pile up while Stuart spent long periods of time in the toilet. One Sunday morning Stuart did not turn up for work. They never saw him again but they read the reports in a local paper concerning a body of a young man found on a gravestone in a local churchyard. Monty's worst fears were confirmed. Drugs were deadly.

"Had you been taking drugs?" he asked.

Monty now held Julian's gaze as his father would have done. He nodded occasionally as Julian sagged between his shoulders and stomach.

"Yes, I thought so," Monty added.

He's weak, Monty, but don't forget that you had a powerful role model that you could emulate. Your father was strong, wasn't he? You never questioned him, Monty, always left your doubts unspoken and when you found a flaw, you could only run away like a coward.

Indeed, Max Brodnitz was a strong man. When he was Julian's age, he found himself on the receiving end of worsening British attitudes to enemy aliens. Churchill ordered internment and Max was soon despatched to Australia with 2000 other refugees. After a period of internment near Sydney, he came back to Britain and joined a Reconnaissance Corp regiment as a Bren Gun Carrier driver. In 1943 he was transferred to the 1st Tank Regiment. "Some people told me I was stupid to want to fight," Max told Monty. "I wanted to do something; I wanted to get my revenge on Hitler and the Nazis for taking my family from me."

As the driver of a Cromwell tank, Max risked his life on many occasions in order to get his revenge on the Nazis. In 1944, he was in action in Normandy and in the Low Countries. Tragedy struck as Max and his unit led the British advance over the Rhine. His tank was hit by an 88mm shell. He and his gunner, Ashley Mead, were the only survivors from a crew of five.

Monty glanced at his watch.

"It's getting late," he said. "Maybe we should continue this discussion tomorrow."

It was working perfectly. Monty knew his father would have been proud of the way he was handling a difficult situation. He recalled the day in 1962 when his father came back from visiting his sick wife at the hospital and said, "So, that is that then. There's just the two of us now. So – who's going to do the cooking?" Monty never told his father that he had heard him - all night long – trying to stifle his pain and tears.

Julian was breathing hard now and his eyes were angled upwards.

"No, dad," he said to the ceiling. "It is not what you think it is."

Monty smothered an angry retort by sipping at his whisky and eyeing his son's face for more clues as to his inner condition. How had this chasm between him and Julian developed like this? Perhaps he, Monty, was to blame. Perhaps he had not shown enough interest. Perhaps he had not been encouraging like his own father had been. Max had been there for him every day and every night until he was old enough to go to university and study the History of Art.

Oh, no, Monty, you are guilty of selected memory or of reconstructing your memories to suit yourself. Your father was not there for you every day and night, was he? Mondays belonged to Max, didn't they? And you never guessed the truth.

Monday was the day Max would disappear into the adult world of pubs, of beer and of darts and laughter. At 18.00 hours precisely, he would head off to Waterloo to spend the evening in The Leather Bottle public house with friends from the war. Monty wondered why his father had used the word "friends" in the plural. Perhaps the use of the plural somehow deflected blame or diverted attention so that Max was able to accept his own behaviour.

One day Monty came back from London during the week. He was looking forward to a father-son evening but he was put out by the presence in his house of a strange man. Stranger still was that it was not on a Monday. Nonetheless, his father was entertaining a friend - in the singular. Max introduced him as his gunner from the war - Ashley Mead. It turned out that Ashley's real name was Heribert Schmidt. A Jew, Heribert had arrived in England in 1938 and joined the British army. He chose the name Ashley because he liked the character Ashley Wilkes from the film *Gone with the Wind.* In 1943, he had joined the 1st Tank Regiment.

Monty turned his head to the world outside. The wind had died down to an occasional sharp gust that barely moved the branches in the trees.

"You said that 'it' was not what I think 'it' is," Monty said to Julian. "Tell me what 'it' is, will you?"

After his first meeting with Ashley, Monty found himself coming back to the house in Wimbledon at odd times in the week. Not a young man given to introspection, he never asked himself why he was doing this. He had a vague notion that he wanted to check that everything at home was as it should be. It never occurred to him that he might be checking up on his father. However, much to his concern, Monty found that Ashley was always in the house.

Julian gasped in surprise and sighed.

"I don't think you are ready to listen, dad."

Monty raised his eyebrows - a signal of his surprise. He had always been a good listener. He listened to Ashley Mead even though Monty knew at the time that this old soldier had somehow seized his role as number-1-man in Max's life.

"I'll write it down, tonight, in a letter. I'll give it to you tomorrow, dad."

Monty nodded. Ashley Mead had never written anything down. Instead, he talked eloquently about his life with Max in the war and he went into much greater detail than his father had ever done. "Why did a soldier fight?" he asked Monty one night. "Why did he endure the deprivations of war, carry on despite mortal danger and put his life at risk? What do you think, Monty? Was it for honour and fame, for freedom, for his country? It was none of these. He fought for his unit, his squad, his crew, his comrades. During operations, the crew lived in and with the tank, not only during combat, but before and after. That meant that the tank was, for the crew, its home and its shelter. In a way that was incomprehensible to outsiders, the crew developed an intimate relationship with its tank and with each other. It was a community born of necessity. Survival was only possible if that community functioned."

Monty knew now that Ashley had been trying to tell him something important. At the time Monty had refused to understand. Even now, he somehow managed to blank this "something important" out in the same way that normal people refused to think about their normal parents having sex.

"But I can tell you this," Julian said: "I am being forced – against my will."

Monty looked up but Julian would not look his father in the eye. He began rubbing at his forehead with thumb and forefinger.

"But I need to tell you something first, dad, about me and my feelings."

He spoke to the floor as though he was ashamed at hearing his own voice and Monty cocked his head and raised his eyebrows but failed to see the fear in his son's eyes.

One day in his third year of university, Monty was at last forced to understand what Ashley had been trying to tell him. He returned home one Monday night. The house was empty. He saw Ashley's clothes in the cloakroom. There were plates and cutlery for two in the kitchen sink. Upstairs there were now two small wardrobes in the bedroom. His father's single bed was now a double and the two dents on the two pillows suggested that two people had been sleeping in it.

And you never confronted Max about it, did you, Monty?

"I'll put it in the letter, but now, let me tell you something about Peter Lutz."

He never dwelt on the significance of this discovery. He never used the word "homosexual". It was forever more a no-go area that Monty refused to contemplate or discuss. Julian had remarked on several occasions that Monty seemed homophobic but each time Monty had refused to engage and simply muttered an obscenity with a shake of the head. Betrayal was something that one never did. He refused to change his view of his father but Max had something unclean inside him as if a cancer had invaded his body that nobody would talk about. This - the unspeakable - lasted much longer than the real cancer, which eventually killed him in 1985.

"Peter Lutz?"

"Yes. Peter Lutz. Our neighbour – remember him? That night at the castle, he was taking pictures."

"What's Peter got to do with all this?"

"Everything. Listen to me, dad, and I'll explain."

12

Friday night/Saturday morning

Monty slapped at the light switch and edged out of the sitting-room and into the darkness. He was no longer sure whether it was late on Friday night or very early on Saturday morning. There was not a glimmer of daybreak and nor was there sight or sound of his son. With a curt "Good night, dad," Julian had left Monty standing by the drinks table in the sitting-room. He was glad of the darkness now. It concentrated his mind and eased the doubts, the concerns and the emotions which tormented him with their contradictions.

The first contradiction concerned Peter Lutz. What Julian had told him was so much at odds with his own experience of the man that, at first, he wondered if he and Julian were talking about the same person. Monty was confused, stunned even. He always had a hard time changing his point of view - especially if he did not want to or if he did not trust the messenger. He liked to think that this reluctance reflected loyalty. His critics called it downright stubbornness. He made the decision there and then to revisit Peter Lutz at the earliest opportunity and to do so with as open a mind as he could muster.

For Monty, Peter Lutz was the quiet neighbour, the polite man he had met in the lawyer's office during the process of buying a part of his land. Their current relationship was partly defined by the polite and formal *Sie* but tempered by the fact that they were both in the antique's business and by the fact that Peter, who had a passion for the English language, usually insisted that they spoke English together. He had learned the language through reading 19th century writers like Thackeray, Dickens and Eliot and their grammatical constructions were often reflected in Peter's conversation. He also had an interest in English idioms, which he often got slightly wrong and caused much merriment. With regard to antiques, he had an unusual speciality - a secret collection that he shared with very few people. One day he had invited Monty to the Villa Rosa in order to see it.

The prospect of sharing this obsession had clearly excited Peter. He chatted about this and that while leading Monty downstairs into the cellar and a poorly lit corridor that barely hid the grime and the dust. Some of this got up Monty's nose and made him sneeze. Peter pushed at a wooden door, flicked at a switch, and drew back a curtain with the sort of flourish Monty associated with stage magicians revealing a lost object or a missing person to an appreciative audience. But instead of the words "Hey presto" Peter said:

"I happened to be in the right place at the right time so I took the bull by a horn and snapped it up."

Monty was about to ask him what he was referring to when, feeling another tickle at the top of his nose, he put out his hand, found something dark and wooden to hold on to and let out one final sneeze. He raised his head and found himself in a large space of uncertain dimensions.

"That is - or was - the door to Hitler's cell after the

failed *Putsch.*"

Monty must have looked confused.

"The door on which you are leaning," Peter said. "It's the entrance to the cell in which he wrote '*Mein Kampf*'."

Monty snatched his hand away as if he was touching something unclean or contaminated. He screwed up his face and examined the door, its heavy iron bolts and its Judas window in the centre.

"I was exceedingly lucky to find myself in the area and jumped at the chance to purchase it," Lutz said.

But Monty had already shifted his attention from the door to a bullet-pocked SS storm trooper's helmet with lightning bolts on the ear flaps. Hundreds of other helmets, mortars and shells, wirelesses and searchlights, all competed for Monty's attention. Rail after rail of uniforms stretched into the distance. They reminded Monty of the Nuremberg Rallies but all in one room.

Unable to tell from Monty's silence whether he was appalled or not, Peter appealed to the one area they had in common - making a profit. The market for Nazi memorabilia, Peter said, had an annual global turnover of more than 500 million dollars. He spent his spare time touring frost-hardened battle sites in Europe and sun-burned battle sites in North Africa, searching for vehicle parts. Peter shrugged.

"This urge to accumulate has been fanatical and excluded demands from my friends and family. Did you know, Herr Brodnitz, that the major auction houses will not handle Nazi memorabilia?"

Monty shook his head.

"No? And if that were not enough," Lutz continued, "eBay has recently prohibited sales on its site."

Peter shrugged again.

"One man's meat is another man's poison," he said and his eyes lit up when he related how he had recently sold a Hitler walking-stick to a Russian collector for more than 5000 Euros.

"Finding buyers outside Germany is not easy," Peter had added. "But the early bird catches worms," and he told Monty about a collector in Dubai who had bought strands of Hitler's hair for 20,000 Euros and a signed copy of *Mein Kampf* for 30.000.

Peter explained how he was trying to set his collection in order, cataloguing late into the night. He had also purchased two barns in the centre of the region and surrounded them with a dozen shipping containers to house his collection.

"Feel free to come and visit," Peter had said. "I would be delighted to show you around."

But several months had passed since that first visit and Monty had yet to take Peter up on his offer.

Monty paused at the bottom of the staircase. Unable to see the top of the stairwell, he put one foot on the bottom stair and started his journey, one step at a time. It was not until he was half way up that his eyes adjusted and he was able to make out the wall at his shoulder. He would have liked to discuss the Lutz problem with Ingrid but he knew she would be sleeping now. Nothing kept her awake. No problem at work was so problematic that it kept her from sleeping. No family disagreement was so disagreeable that it disturbed her night's rest. Monty envied her. He was too busy absorbing the conversation with Julian to even ask himself whether he was tired or not. His son had marched off to bed and left Monty stranded by the drinks table, dealing with intrusions from his own past, by a variety of allegations and by these contradictions now making his head spin.

In a tone Monty judged to be non-accusatory he had confronted Julian about his participation in the riot during the week. Perhaps the word "confronted" was inappropriate. Perhaps he had been running scared from

Julian's questions about Daniela, running scared from Julian's story about Peter Lutz. Monty tripped over the top stair and landed heavily on his knee. Cursing his own clumsiness, he limped into the bathroom wondering why Julian's responses had caught him right off his guard. On top of that, he was teased by doubts about Julian's version of the riot and his role in it. He even doubted his own recollections. They seemed to change each time he accessed his memory.

He undressed, threw his clothes into the wash basket and stood naked in front of the full-length mirror. Uncluttered and free, he stared at himself. Was this the reflection of a man who could not accept his own father and, by extension, his own son, as Julian had suggested? He waited for an answer but there was just the faraway clackety-clack of a runaway train racing through the night. He tried a question from a different angle. Was this the reflection of a man guilty of judging those he should love by a code of morals that belonged to an era that predated the Beatles? Monty listened for a reply but all he heard was the soft shuffling sound of a house full of sleep.

He made his way along the corridor to the bedroom. He skirted the area where he had stubbed his toe earlier in the day. He glowered in the direction of the old suitcase and then stopped to peer at it. It had always housed the Christmas decorations, but there was no denying the fact that it was no longer there. Ingrid had removed it along with its contents. When Monty had first seen the case, over 20 years previously, it was with the eye of the antique dealer. He looked askance at it and could not understand why anyone would want to hold on to such a worthless object. Now, despite his sore toe, Monty felt he had lost a childhood friend. It was the sort of suitcase that might contain old letters or diaries and secrets. There might be tales telling of life in the

Sudetenland before the expulsions. There might be accounts of life as refugees and stories like the ones that Ingrid had told him. The truth, however, was that the suitcase contained nothing but the fears, the doubts and the dreams of the refugees themselves.

Now, standing in the darkness of a timeless zone late at night, Monty saw that those dreams had escaped from the suitcase like genies from a bottle and now lived and breathed in the real world. The children and grandchildren of the refugees were their dreams. The words "family" and "tree" Monty mused, had been well chosen. If Ingrid and Julian were the tree then the roots of the tree were the dreams of Oma Gretl and Opa Siegfried. That meant his wife and son were the embodiment of the hopes of two people he had never met. From this perspective, Monty understood why Ingrid had to face her parents, to forgive them for being refugees and to show them what had become of their concerns. "Look at me and look at your grandson," she might say. "Everything has turned out fine. There is nothing to worry about."

Making his way along the corridor, Monty wondered whether he and Julian were the embodiment of his father Max's dreams. Did Max really deserve such a narrow-minded son as Montgomery Bradley? Did Monty deserve such a man as Max as a father?

Monty had lost all sense of time. He could not remember how long it had been since the church clock had last chimed. Slipping between the sheets, he glanced at the luminous hands of the bedside clock. It was two o'clock. A mound next to him and a shape on the pillow told him that Ingrid was sleeping. He pulled the blankets up to his chin and rolled over. He looked again at the illuminated digital clock and closed his eyes. There was a twinkling, swirling pattern of stars and colours - a sort of make-shift light show on the inside of Monty's closed eyelids. He tried to blink it away but this visual phenomenon, this light-induced afterimage of what he had seen, continued. He blinked again but the flash of light was still there and it was bringing images from the riot flashing into his consciousness.

First was the image of someone in a Klu Klux Klan outfit stretched out on the pavement in front of a bus to block any attempt it might make to leave. Other white-robed figures were carrying metal pipes, clubs, and chains, and they were milling around the bus while others looked on and shouted.

"Dirty foreigners."

"Sieg Heil."

Monty knew he was not recalling the events in the correct order. The memories seemed to come randomly and he was surprised because each memory appeared to him like a photograph rather than a moving film. Nothing was moving unless he decided to set the scene in motion by activating it himself.

It was the shock of the event that Monty experienced first and he still felt it as a question mark on his forehead and slight palpitations in his neck. He could not recall any prediction or forewarning of the violence. *Tannenheim* had not been alive with rumours that a mob planned to greet the arrival of the refugees at the castle. Further, there was no reason to believe that their arrival would spark off a spontaneous riot of aggression and death. Nobody in *Tannenheim* had mentioned their upcoming arrival with threats of violence. Nobody he knew had been organising active resistance. References were made to the *Vaterlaendische Front* but these references were received with the twist of a smile that indicated something that was not to be taken as more than a joke.

It was only now, two days afterwards, that he was putting his memories into some kind of logical order. He was troubled by the idea that the act of remembering was rendered inaccurate by his own post-event knowledge, by wishful thinking and by what Julian was now bringing to the story. This last was particularly complicated. Sometimes he believed his son. A minute later and Monty would curse himself for allowing Julian to corrupt his memories.

The police for example, were newcomers to Monty's memory. Introduced by Julian no more than one hour before, they were placed in the castle forecourt and standing over the refugees. These were lying or sitting in a daze a few yards from the shell of the bus. Nobody seemed in a hurry to call an ambulance. Monty now knew that several refugees had inhaled smoke and fumes and were in serious need of medical attention. It would be some time before any of them saw a doctor. One of them was going to die. But he had not known that at the time.

A crazed individual brought a crowbar smashing through one of the side windows of the bus. While one group of men rocked the vehicle in a vain attempt to turn it on its side, a second tried to enter through the front door. For the next few minutes, the mob pounded on the bus bellowing at the refugees to come out and to take what they deserved. But they stayed in their seats.

"Burn them alive," the demonstrators screamed.

"Fry the bastards."

When several choking people crawled away from the bus a figure in a white robe, a figure introduced by Julian just an hour ago, rushed forward, rested a hand on a choking man's shoulder and seemed about to help. Another man rushed forward with a baseball bat as the rest of the exiting refugees spilled out onto the grass. The white-robed figure was pushed aside.

Two bodies were then pulled from the bus. They fell to the floor and tried to shield themselves from further

102

attack. The mob pounded them. While a pair of individuals lifted heads, others punched them until the individuals lost consciousness. One frenzied assailant continued to stomp on a man's chest. The figure in the white robes was there again and stepping in to call a halt to the beating.

Someone ran toward the bus and tossed a flaming bundle of rags through a broken window. Within seconds the bundle exploded, sending dark gray smoke throughout the bus. Monty thought he heard a shout:

"They are going to burn us."

Monty was not given to wild imagining but surely such a shout would have been in Arabic and yet, he was sure he had heard it in German. Had he, perhaps, heard the words in his own mind?

A head appeared through an open window gasping for air. Seconds later, three individuals squeezed through the windows and dropped to the ground. Still choking from the smoke and fumes, they staggered across the castle forecourt. Several other passengers had escaped through the front door of the bus. The figure in the white robe was there to help them. And then the hood was removed. It was Julian's face – not laughing but crying for the others to stop.

As Monty drifted towards sleep, he wondered how much detail had already faded away and lay beyond his grasp and how much detail had been added since he had witnessed the scene. Was there nobody he could trust? Monty found consolation by reminding himself that only retrospect could bring order to events and you needed special people to do that and these special people were called historians. Furthermore, Monty knew only too well that age brought a tendency to see the darker side of life and that the world was never as bad as he tended to expect. You simply needed to talk your problems through with a trusted friend, Monty thought. But his trusted friend could not be woken now and even if he did shake her shoulder and rouse her, the thought of telling her that her husband had been spying on their son made him tearful.

He closed his eyes and tried to find sleep, tried to ignore the threat of silence, the imaginings and the memory of Julian's voice telling him that this was the 21st century and pleading with him to be himself. "Yes, I was there, dad, but I tried to help those poor people. Decide for yourself what is right and wrong."

13

Saturday – early morning

"How good you are getting up so early, Monty. Thank you so very much."

Monty smiled a response, let out the clutch and turned into *Tannenheim's* main street. At first, he saw only spirals of mist swimming in the air but when he passed the baker's he saw human shapes and shadows under the street lamps. The shapes were shrugged and huddled against the cold and flicking their heads in his direction as he passed. He changed up a gear and accelerated towards the traffic lights glowing red in the distance. Inclining his head towards the passenger seat, he said:

"So – put me in the picture."

"Which picture, Monty?"

Monty sucked in air between his teeth. It was sometimes easy to forget that Ingrid was not a native speaker of such an idiomatic language as English.

"You said you'd tell me why you need to do this," Monty said.

"Forgive my parents? You want to change my mind?"

Monty shook his head.

"I'm not going to argue with you," he said to her reflection in the windscreen. "I just want to know why now."

Monty pulled up at the traffic light and tugged at the handbrake. Six o'clock on a cold November morning was indeed early but this end of the main street was full of commuters jostling on the pavement and hurrying to catch the next tram from *Bahnhofstrasse*. The railway station had long since been replaced by the tram-stop but like much else in *Tannenheim*, the history of the town was present in the names of buildings whose original purposes were long since defunct. The Old Forge and the Old Bakery were now private houses while the Slaughterhouse had been converted into a community centre. When Monty had been a newcomer to *Tannenheim*, he was obliged, on occasions, to ask directions. Local people would say things like, "Go down the street to where the bank used to be" or "Turn left where the butcher was." Much to Monty's surprise and despite the fact that, by 1942, the Villa Rosa had been emptied of its Brodnitz occupants, many of the townsfolk still referred to it as "the Brodnitz residence." It seemed that "Brodnitz" was a well-remembered name and not only in the *Stolperstein* but also in a children's playground nearby called "*Brodnitz Anlage*."

"Why now?" Ingrid said.

"Yes, you were always set against the idea."

Monty accelerated away from the lights and followed the blue *Autobahn* sign along the "mountain road."

"Change, perhaps?"

"Brought on by what?"

"What happened to the refugees."

"You mean the ones at the castle?"

Ingrid nodded and then shook her head again. Wiping at her nose, she blew noisily through her teeth.

"I have often dreamed that my parents came to me to explain themselves. This is not going to happen now. So - to honour my dreams I will have to go to them."

"But..."

"You see, don't you, Monty, what happened at the castle has helped me understand."

"Understand?"

"Why they betrayed me. I have to tell them this before they die."

So, that's it. Wednesday's tragedy at the castle has rekindled both an interest in, and sympathies with, her own family's tragedy at the end of World War 2.

Monty remained silent, musing on the power of the past, the power of family and the cyclical nature of life's journey. Many people he knew had spent the first half of their lives breaking away from their parents and their roots only to spend the second half trying to find their way back. If they ever found a way back, their parents were often long gone. Ingrid was lucky. Her parents were still alive.

Perhaps it was this cyclical nature of life that had moved him to build their house on land that had once belonged to the house in which his own father had been brought up. It had never once crossed Monty's mind that this was his attempt to make amends, his attempt to tell his father that he had never rejected him and that he was sorry for his behaviour. The fact that the Villa Rosa had a recent history that was, at best, ambiguous, had never entered his head.

The house had been taken over by the Nazis and used as a hospital for the duration of the war. For many years afterwards, it had been used as a rehabilitation centre. In 1958, Peter Lutz's father, Oscar, had bought the Villa Rosa at a knock-down rate. The locals rarely mentioned

Oscar Lutz and if they did, mention of the name was accompanied by the sort of disapproving silence that usually prefaced topics like "paedophilia" or "Stalingrad." One day, Peter Lutz had surprised Monty by being the first *Tannenheim* resident to tell Monty about his father's involvement in the war.

Born in 1914, Oscar would have had trouble avoiding it. He served with the *SS-Standarte Germania* in the Polish campaign of 1939 and was awarded the Iron Cross for bravery in action. In August 1940, he received a commission in the Waffen-SS. He saw plenty of action in Russia and was decorated again in August 1942. In December 1943, he was sent to the Leningrad front as a *Sturmbannfuhrer* - the equivalent of major - and held the position until he was wounded in July 1944 while defending a hill against a massive Russian onslaught.

After his recovery, he joined the SS Panzer Brigade Westfalen, which was sent immediately to counter the US Rhine crossing at Remagen. Too little, too late, the attempt to counter the Americans was doomed from the start and Major Lutz found himself on a variety of operations in Germany until he was captured by GIs and sent to a special SS internment camp near Frankfurt where he stayed for two years.

On his release from the internment camp, he found that the Cold War brought unexpected opportunities. His numerous contacts brought him in touch with NATO operatives, who were impressed by his wartime experiences. For many years he worked as an Intelligence Operative in Darmstadt. After that job had run its course, Lutz found lucrative work as a representative for a construction company. By 1958, he had saved enough money to buy the Villa Rosa - only 13 years after the war's end.

Whatever he was doing, Lutz never lost touch with his former SS comrades. *Tannenheim* residents were laconic on the topic but, by putting together the information he had gathered, Monty was able to build up a picture of the regular reunions held at the Villa Rosa. Peter Lutz remembered that the meetings allowed old comrades who had "shared their last crust of bread together during the war" simply to keep in touch. Politics were never discussed and the singing of Waffen-SS marching songs was done out of alcoholic nostalgia. Peter said that until his father's death in 1984, the walls of the Villa Rosa would shake to renditions of: *"Auf der Heide blüht ein kleines Blümelein, und das heisst Erika,"* while *"Ich hatte einen Kameraden"* was sung at the end of the evening in order to remember "absent friends."

Monty glanced through the car's side window. A suggestion of sunlight was glowing behind the hills of the *Niebelungwald.* Ingrid said:

"Mum was 10 years old and dad was 12 when they were forced to leave their homes, their friends and their families in Sudetenland."

Monty glanced at his watch. It was 6.45. He braced himself. He was half-expecting Ingrid to embark on a performance of that epic tale of her dispossessed people. When he and Ingrid had first met, she had rarely mentioned these stories and oral traditions and he had known little of the history of the *Sudetentland* Germans or what had happened to them at the war's end. Then, one day, shortly after Julian was born, Monty watched Ingrid while she bottle-fed their baby. She had turned to look towards the window. Her head was raised and she stared into the darkness outside as if she was remembering. Then, she looked down at the baby, curved over him and recited the narrative of her mother and father as if it were a nursery rhyme.

After that, she often told Monty stories and she used story-telling techniques that were typical of the oral traditions that characterised two of Monty's favourite tales - the *Iliad* and the *Odyssey*. Ingrid's style was full of rhetorical questions, and her repetition of phrases and names was designed to involve the audience and to aid memory. Monty had a role to play and it was not to argue with her.

"And your mum's mum - Oma Gretl - was alone at this time, wasn't she?"

Ingrid pulled at her pony tail and held on to it with both hands while looking through the windscreen.

"Yes, her husband, Rainer, had been killed in Russia in 1943."

"And Opa Siegfried's wife died on the trek to Germany, right?"

"Right. She died in Germany actually - in the camp for refugees at Pirna."

"Typhus?"

She nodded and turned her head towards her side window. Monty pulled off the mountain road, accelerated along the slip and onto the motorway. Glancing into the rear-view mirror he saw that the light was glowing brighter behind the hills but the sun had not yet risen and the forest was still just a silhouette against the skyline. Monty knew the forest so well he could almost smell the rotting wood, the smell of fresh earth when the day was not quite day.

The history of the *Niebelungwald* was, like that of the town, present in its place names: the copse named "Seven Sisters," and the "Kaiser Oak." There was also a memorial stone just behind *Tannenberg Schloss* and erected in memory of twelve escaped prisoners shot by the SS just before the war's end. Above it all, out of sight but not out of mind, was the *Tannenheim Kreuz* - soon to be lighting the way for lost travellers.

"It must have been traumatic for them - your parents, I mean."

Ingrid shook her head in disbelief.

"My mum thinks Oma Gretl was raped - but Oma never talked about it. She was always a bit neurotic - you know, fearful of everything and everybody. What unkindness mum and dad experienced I can hardly imagine. No wonder they were afraid of the authorities. No wonder they wanted to keep their noses clean."

"Given the record of both the Czechs and the Russians after the war," Monty said, "I'm not surprised they were fearful."

With regard to the immediate post-war period in Europe, Monty now considered himself quite knowledgeable. He knew that in the aftermath of World War 2, the Czechoslovak state had been restored, and the government had expelled the majority of ethnic Germans. The decision to expel was taken on the grounds that the behaviour of the Sudetenland Germans had been a major cause of the war. But Monty believed that Czech policy was opportunistic and he saw it as nothing less than ethnic cleansing.

"But your Oma Gretl and Opa Siegfried settled in Germany, didn't they?"

Ingrid shook her head.

"Not really. Temporariness was a feeling they never threw off. They thought that one day they would go back home. Some of the survivors hang on to this belief even now."

Except, Monty knew, "even now" was pointless. In 2013, the Czech President Elect, Petr Necas, had made it clear that although his country regretted the forcible expulsion of Sudeten Germans and the injustice inflicted upon innocent people, the door was closed to property claims raised by deported Germans.

They were nearing the airport now. Monty detected it in the smell of jet fuel, the thrum of engines at takeoff, the vibration of the plane while it waited before releasing its brakes and hurtling down the runway. Images of exotic places and their promise of freedom flashed through his consciousness. Monty loved airports.

"And their children, your parents," he prompted, "Waltraud and Kurt - they settled, didn't they?"

Ingrid nodded.

"In practical terms they were young enough to fully integrate. They never had that temporary mindset. They saw themselves as Germans - in large part because Germany finally started seeing them as Germans and not refugees. I feel guilty now. They must have been afraid that they would be deported again - that my juvenile agitation and behaviour would bring them to the attention of the authorities."

A distant emergency vehicle, siren screaming, forced Ingrid to pause. Then she said:

"Please, let me tell the story about my dad. He..."

"You can't blame yourself."

"For my dad?"

"No. You can't blame yourself for what your family did to you."

"So, who is to blame?"

"Maybe nobody was to blame."

"Oh, come on, Monty. I was not ignorant. There was an informal club for the refugees. It later became the *Bund der Vetriebenen* - the League of Refugees. I knew what had gone on after the war."

"The League still exists, right?"

Ingrid nodded.

"When we were young, Dieter and I would go to the League's meetings. Sooner or later someone would begin a dialogue with the others and another story of heartache and fear would unfold. In the beginning, the stories served a useful purpose by maintaining the identity of the *Bund's* members and binding them together. It was a sort of therapy."

"More than just a talking shop, then."

"*Absolut*. You can understand why dad was upset when I began my little political protest. He and mum must've thought I had gone off the rails, as you say, and that I was breaking the law. I don't blame my parents for going to the police. What would you do, Monty, if you knew Julian had broken the law? Surely, you would have no option but to go to the Police, wouldn't you?"

Monty concentrated on the exit slip and the cars now coming at him from all directions.

"Do you think they regret it?" Monty ventured to ask.

Ingrid swung round to face him.

"Regret betraying me? Of course, they regret it," she said.

"Really? Are you sure?"

Ingrid took a sharp intake of breath and spoke with a snap to her voice.

"Of course, I am sure. I'm a parent, too, remember?"

"I wasn't criticising," Monty said.

"I didn't say you were, Monty. Now listen. We only have a few minutes. I'm now going to tell you a story about my dad."

Monty pulled up at a traffic light. They were only a short distance from the drop-off point. He shook himself and smiled his presence into her eyes.

"And I can tell you now," she said, "that you have never heard this story before."

14

Saturday – early morning

Monty was leaning forward, his head almost touching the windscreen, when he signalled and shot into the free space outside departures. His heart was racing in a way it often did in the airport drop-off zone.

"Made it," he said, switching off the engine and glancing at the activity around him.

Underneath the appearance of normality, there was a feeling of excitement, anticipation and impatience. Some people were dragging suitcases through the revolving doors, some were standing on the pavement and listening to MP3s or playing video games while others were grabbing a last smoke in the reserved areas. There were also those who seemed bemused - caught in a twilight zone between arrival and departure. Stranded in no-man's-land, these travellers blinked at the world passing them by until the plane came to take them away to their final destination.

Don't be so cynical, Monty. These are the very people who leave items behind them, aren't they? These are the people you have made a good living from.

"So - why have I never heard this story before?"

Monty wound down the window to allow fresh air to circulate in the car's interior. He heard snippets of talk from people passing their car, a quick exchange about the weather in New York, the possibility of rain and concerns about terrorism. Ingrid said:

"Partly because I had disowned my father and I wanted everyone else to do the same."

"Partly?"

"And partly because many of the stories I tell are probably myths - the result of collective memory."

"Fabrications, you mean?"

A smell of scent wafted through the car window and followed its owner like a vapour trail through the automatic door. Monty sniffed at the fading odour and tried to identify it: *Chanel* or *Burberry*? The automatic door had failed and now stood wide open. Through it came the whir of wheels on the marbled terminal floor, a voice on the Tannoy system announcing that flight 233 was ready for boarding and a reminder that unaccompanied luggage would be taken away and destroyed. Monty was reflecting on the repercussions this no-nonsense policy might have on the Lost Property business when Ingrid said:

"No, not fabrications. But you have to understand, Monty, that..."

But Monty was away with a variety of noises. There were the voices of young and old - the subdued tones of anticipated separation, the excited tones of the anticipated holiday in the sun. And accompanying the voices was the seasonal music marking the arrival of Christmas. Suitcases were hauled across the pavement and dumped on trolleys. Occasionally, Monty heard the roar of an aeroplane taking off or landing. Not unkindly, Ingrid said:

"Close the window, Monty."

"You'd better get a move on," Monty said nodding towards a parking attendant. The attendant held his pad of penalty stickers at the ready and he was moving in Monty and Ingrid's direction.

"And you need to remember that I wasn't born until 1966. This means that my Sudetenland stories are mostly based on the accounts of Oma Gretl and Opa Siegfried and reinforced by their children, Kurt and Waltraud. These stories have surely been embellished by the memories of other members of the *Bund der Vetriebenen.* Many of us, the grandchildren, have adopted these stories as our own."

"But not this story?"

"No, not this story."

A taxi entered the drop-off zone and screeched to a halt. The driver beeped his horn and gesticulated in Monty's direction.

"Ignore him," Ingrid said. "And listen to me. Did you know that dad was never able to say *danke schoen?* Imagine going through life without so much as a 'Thank you.' Dad nodded his thanks and said it with his face. Even now, whenever I say *danke schoen* I think of my dad. Let me tell you why."

"Yes, do," Monty said, conscious both of the advancing parking attendant and of the dark looks he and Ingrid were drawing from other taxi drivers.

"You have five minutes, Monty. Don't let them bully you."

Ingrid paused and stared at Monty as if expecting something. He shook himself. In this oral narrative, he had an important prompting role to play.

"When did it all happen?"

"It was evening at the end of April, 1946," Ingrid said, switching to German on the word "end." "A house burned down about 500 metres from home."

"Whose home, Ingrid?"

"Kurt and Waltraud's home. My parents' home."

"Who saw all this, Ingrid?"

"My father, Kurt, he saw it all. He was just a boy."

"What did he see?"

"He saw the Czech police come into the village."

"What did they want?"

"They took all the men of the village and gathered them in the square."

"How many men?"

"Over one hundred of them. Kurt heard the police telling the men to get down on their knees."

"Why did they do that?"

"They said the villagers were responsible for the fire."

"But they were not responsible."

"No, but Kurt watched the police beat the men to a bloody mess with their truncheons and rifle butts."

Monty shivered. He had become aware of a gradual change in the quality of Ingrid's voice. It was in the clipping of words and in the sound of the vowels. There was no doubt about it, she was speaking German with a slight Sudetenland accent. In a sense she was assuming another identity and it brought goose bumps to Monty's skin.

"I don't want to hurry you," Monty said, "but we don't have much time."

Monty glanced through the windscreen. Four cars away, the parking attendant was slipping a ticket under the windscreen wiper.

"Ingrid?"

"After a while the officer in charge decided to have some fun," she said. "He told the men that he had been ordered to kill those responsible for the fire but he was going to spare their lives. He said he wanted to hear the men thank him."

"And what did the men do?"

117

"They said '*danke schoen*.''Louder,' the officer said. '*Danke schoen*,' the men said. 'Louder,' said the officer. '*Danke schoen*' they said."

"Was that the end?"

"No, that wasn't the end. The officer and his subordinates proceeded to beat the men again. These, the men of the village, were people Kurt had been brought up to respect. They were his elders and betters. It was the sound of their breaking noses that he never forgot - a muffled snap, like the breaking of a large celery stick and followed by '*danke schoen*' and a gush of blood."

Ingrid stopped suddenly and stared in front of her as though seeing and hearing. Her eyelids dropped like blinds and she shook her head. She snapped the door open and marched towards the parking attendant. Monty watched Ingrid's finger waving between arched eyebrows, then pointing at the car and finally jabbing at her watch. The attendant raised his hand to his cap and Ingrid came back to the car.

"We don't know what these experiences did to these people," she said, slamming the door. "They did not ask for it. They had to live with it for the rest of their lives. You know, Monty, these psychological scars passed themselves on to the next generation like the stories they told. It was like a genetic condition. Kurt and Waltraud had it in their bodies when they were born."

"What exactly is 'it'?" Monty asked.

"Fear," Ingrid said. "Fear of the authorities, fear of doing the wrong thing. Fear dictated their thinking and their behaviour. It is not their fault, but this fear has to stop somewhere. And I am the one to do it."

"How?"

"By forgiveness," Ingrid said. "Only then will the scars disappear forever."

Without waiting for Monty to respond, Ingrid pushed open the door, walked round to the back of the car and opened the hatch. She said:

"I want your problem with Julian sorted by the time I get back."

Monty spread his hands and opened his mouth to tell her that the process was underway but Ingrid raised her hand in order to silence him.

"I don't want to be rude, Monty, but..."

Monty braced himself. As good as her English was, she had never mastered that polite rudeness at which the English were so adept.

"Just do it, Monty. And don't be too hard on him. Remember that he is your only son. You won't get another chance. He loves you but you will lose him like my parents lost me."

While Ingrid fumbled with her trolley, Monty pulled an envelope from the back pocket of his jeans. He had found it propped up against the whisky bottle in the sitting-room that very morning. He knew immediately that it was the letter Julian said he would write. Monty ran lightly pinched fingers along the top of the envelope. He was unsure whether it was the time to open it he had to find or the courage to read it. If it were courage, his behaviour was in marked contrast to the bravery he was witnessing now. Ingrid's pony tail was swinging confidently behind her when she turned to wave at him. By the time she arrived at the departures board, her hand was fumbling in her handbag and her head was flicking nervously from side to side as if she was suffering from a nervous tic. It embarrassed Monty to think that he was thinking about himself whereas Ingrid was already back in Berlin, and looking for an answer to a question that had haunted her for over 25 years.

It was on the way home that Monty stopped at a service station and took Julian's letter out of his back pocket. Inserting his finger into the top corner of the envelope, Monty sliced it open and slid the letter out.

Dear dad

Here is the letter I said I would write. I feel that a letter is the best way to get across what I feel about our relationship. So how is life? How is the business doing? What have you been up to this year? I finished my IB exams last summer and now study in the same city you work in. But enough small talk.

Some time ago, I came to see you in your office and I saw you with another woman in a restaurant. Who was she, dad? She was all over you and I could not help noticing that you did nothing to stop it. And you looked so happy. I can't stand by and watch my family destroy itself but what am I supposed to do? Tell my mum or protect her from the truth? Stop you from having an affair? Stop these secrets? Erase this mistake? I realise that I cannot do any one of these things.

A couple of weeks ago I decided to face you. I thought we could have lunch together and talk about it but outside your building I couldn't bring myself to take the last few steps and knock on the door.

What if I had knocked on the door? Would you have welcomed me or would you have treated me like an unwelcome visitor? Perhaps you would have left me hovering outside, exchanging empty words without saying anything real. How did we get into this situation? I realised then that the problem is not just the other woman, dad. There has been nothing much between us for some time. I've wanted to write a letter like this for years. To be honest, I suppose that I was waiting for you to make the first move. I can be too optimistic sometimes. After our conversation a couple of hours ago, I decided sit down and compose my thoughts.

I'm writing because I have questions. I'm writing because I have complaints. I'm writing because one of us has to take the initiative to shatter the wall of silence that separates us. And I need your help in dealing with Peter L. But even as I make this effort to do the right thing, I wonder if I'm wasting my time.

I want to understand, for instance, why you never call me. I am trying to understand why you never visit me at university. I am trying to understand why you never ask me how I am getting on. The thing I'm trying to understand the most is how you can be so distant when you say you were so close to your own father. Or were you as close as you think? He was gay, wasn't he, dad, and my guess is that you can't admit it to yourself. Is that why you cannot accept that I am gay, too? All I have are theories. You'll have to give me your take on why our relationship has gone downhill. I wonder, though, whether you understand your own motives. Do you?

I have the right to be upset. Who would not be upset watching the family tear itself apart? And I have the right to demand answers. You haven't given me much in the last few years but you could at least give me help through these difficult times. Still, I wonder if anything that I am writing matters to you. Honestly, I can see you reading this letter and tossing it into the rubbish bin. There is so much I want to tell you about me but I don't know how to get through to you.

My mum and I sat around the table trying to work out why I had felt unable to knock on your door that day. While I sat there, I felt so much resentment against you because by not telling mum about you, I was, in a way, complicit in your unfaithfulness. I think, perhaps subconsciously, I was saving myself the grief of your response.

Can you understand my feelings of frustration? In our previous conversations, which ended abruptly, as you were needed at work, I'd ask you how you were doing with business and you talked about the weather. No one listening in would have been able to tell there was any difference between our relationship and one you might have with a neighbour.

I know you are busy at work and that you have to pay for the house. Is that why you never came to my school graduation? Didn't you know that I would have liked you to be there? I am now in trouble, dad, and I need you now like I never needed you before.

According to Mum, I make similar jokes to yours and I try to swallow the lump in my throat when she laughs and says I've inherited my sense of humour from you.

Maybe she does it to keep alive the connection to the slight relationship that exists between us.

Perhaps the reason I didn't knock on your door that time was that I just don't care anymore. If you can betray the family, why should I believe in you? I'm exhausted trying to make this work. Maybe a part of me wasn't actually bothered whether I saw you or not that day – you've already lost so much meaning in my life; you are someone who signs the birthday card that mum buys.

You haven't given me much to hold on to. Perhaps the light has been dimming for a long time and it is only now that I realise the light is turned off. With you spending most of your time at work, maybe we never had a chance to build a relationship. So, is it safe to say let's call it a day? Clearly you can't give me what I need and, unlike you, I'm actually doing perfectly well with mum.

This isn't me being bitter, although I was initially. It's just a way of telling you how I really feel without being dismissed.

Last night I explained what happened at the castle and I explained that control that Peter Lutz has over me. There is nothing we can do about my sexual orientation, dad, but we can do something about Lutz, can't we?

Your son

J

15

Saturday – late afternoon

The sun was already sinking behind the Villa Rosa when the front door of his house swung open and Monty emerged in the twilight. He loitered in the driveway, zipped up his leather jacket, kicked his heels at the gate and looked up and down the street as though expecting someone to turn up at any moment. It was warm for the time of year, as Ingrid had suggested, but the light mist, now thickening in the autumn dusk, had been cold enough to put him off the idea of a bike ride earlier in the afternoon.

With his shoulders tightening against the dampness, he slipped his fingers into the back pocket of his jeans and pulled out Julian's letter. Then he checked the mailbox, stepped over to the paper-waste bin and dropped the junk mail into it. He was about to throw the letter into the bin with the junk mail, hesitated and slid it back into the pocket of his jeans. He turned into the street and looked towards the entrance to the Villa Rosa.

It was getting dark and the glow of an autumn moon was visible through the spruces and silver firs that lined the hilltops. On the lower slopes, where the forest neared the town, a breeze was stripping the deciduous trees of their remaining leaves. Monty heard the breeze rushing up the main street towards him, skirting the Villa Rosa and whooshing through the forest, picking up the branches of the trees and knocking them together with a clack, clack, clack.

Monty allowed himself a shiver of agitation when he saw a light burning in the Villa Rosa. He then blew out his cheeks and set off along the pavement. To focus himself, he picked his way along the curb lintels, arms waving in the manner of a tightrope walker, while he tried to keep his feet from straying onto the road or the paving stones. He told himself that if he could keep a straight line then the ensuing confrontation with Peter Lutz would go to his advantage. If he put a foot wrong then disaster would strike. Julian would be revealed as a liar and Monty would find himself the father of a murderer.

The shared history of the Villa Rosa and Monty's house was memorialised in the low picket fence that divided the two plots and by the shared decorative brick wall that separated both properties from the street. The wall had been constructed from white and red bricks from a now-defunct local brick factory, but Monty gave no thought to its style while he approached Peter's house. Its entrance was signalled by a recess in the wall and wrought-iron double gates painted in blue. Monty tried to ignore the trip stones in the recess. The purpose of his visit was to deal with the present and future. A vain hope when the night encouraged people to consider the past. In the darkness, the memory of his paternal grandmother rose up to greet him. *Ida Brodnitz: born Benjamin, 1898, deported 1942, murdered 16.09.1942 in Theresienstadt.*

Monty's father had rarely talked of leaving his family

in Germany in 1939. It had always been a sort of no-man's-land around which the boy Monty tiptoed. And on those rare occasions when his father did talk about it, Monty realised that the words he used were always the same words and they were sounds in a vacuum; dead things that his father had disconnected from his feelings.

"The worst thing that ever happened to me was leaving my mother at the station," Max intoned. "She was crying and wasn't allowed on the platform. I don't remember much of that. I think I've wiped it from my mind. I was just crying, crying, crying. And I'm still crying."

And if he could manage it, Max would add:

"Six million Jews were slaughtered. My parents, uncles and aunts all died in concentration camps. I hate seeing images of those times. I hate it. It makes me feel sick."

Max was a little more forthcoming about his first year in England. On arrival, he spoke little English and nobody spoke German or tried to speak slowly or understand him.

"People ask you 'How do you feel to be in England?' and you want to tell them you feel disjointed, displaced, distressed, disappointed but you don't have these words to explain yourself. So, you just shrug and say you don't know or 'I'm fine'."

At other times Max would say:

"It is incredible how big your problems are when you are homeless in a strange city."

Max would sometimes elaborate and reveal that in those early days, he understood what alienation was.

"To a Londoner, the names "Waterloo" "Oxford Street," and "Clapham" were as familiar as their own fingers and toes and they expected the same from others. If they did not get it, they treated you with suspicion. All I wanted was to be a normal human being with a job and to be reunited with my family."

Monty had never seen his father as anything but a true Englishman. He certainly never associated him with the word "refugee." Fathers were not supposed to be weak, thankful, helpless refugees. It was only when Ashley Mead came into Monty's life that he began to understand.

"We are both refugees," Max had explained. "We are both German. We have had similar experiences here as refugees and as soldiers. We speak the same mother tongue and we have the same everyday cultural reference points: the colour and shape of a post-box, the names of shops, of food, and popular songs and radio programmes. We understand each other perfectly."

Outside the double gates, Monty was listening to his father's voice, feeling his father's emotions as if Max's life and his joys and fears were within him - a part of his very fabric. Monty frisked himself and plunged his hand into the back pockets of his jeans. He fingered the letter and felt some comfort at the touch of it. Monty had read it through several times, was still absorbing the letter's contents.

Monty admitted that he had never received such a critical letter - not even from his teachers at Wimbledon Grammar School for boys. His first instinct had been to throw the thing away, to rid himself of the feelings of inadequacy and failure that the criticism had sparked off. He had kept the letter along with his feelings. But maybe there was something there that could be rescued, some points of compromise that might lead to the beginnings of a new relationship with his son. Monty slid his hand against the jeans just to reassure himself that the letter was still there, shrugged all feelings away and told himself to focus on his current purpose. It was Peter Lutz he had come to see and Julian he had come to talk about. He had promised Ingrid that he would deal with it.

Monty passed through the double gates and stood several metres from the front door of the Villa Rosa. The driveway was cobbled in a fan pattern and the front steps rising from it were flanked by a capped wall. The front door was panelled and divided into six sections; the top panels filled with cut glass. The door gleamed with brass knobs and knockers.

Monty walked up the steps, looked up and around at the hidden sky, the silhouettes of the trees, and then at the door-knocker - a heavy ring hinged in the mouth of a lion's head. Monty took a deep breath and lifted his hand. He grabbed at the knocker as if it would stop him from falling. The fact was that his heart was doing another balancing act in his neck. It was worse than usual and Monty had the uncomfortable sensation that darkness was permeating his head and sinking downwards in the manner of a spreading ink blot.

Monty took another deep breath, pulled the ring back and struck the plate below the lion's head, once, twice. He stepped backwards and waited. The strike on the plate had set up a humming thump that rolled away inside the house. When it became clear that the front door was going to remain firmly shut, Monty turned and skipped down the steps. He fully intended to go straight back to his own house but almost against his will he turned down the side of the Villa Rosa. While his feet crunched on the gravel, Monty experienced that bite at the guts, the need to empty his bowels that the unfamiliar frequently provoked. He was about to enter a part of the Villa grounds that was unknown to him. This side of the house was invisible from Monty's house; it was the dark side of the moon, the secret garden that had retained its privacy.

In contrast, the strip of land nearest to his house was clearly visible from Monty's fish-bowl lounge and

Monty often sat in his favourite chair and contemplated it. He imagined he saw house guests walking along paths that ran between flower-beds bordered by low hedges. Tea was carried by servants across the lawns to people sitting in wicker chairs under the branches of the old oak tree. He even imagined his grandmother, Ida Brodnitz, dressed in green coat and skirt, and an apron with pockets for knives and twine.

The secret garden, on the other hand, was a tangle of shrubbery in the darkness. Half-seen paths and low walls ran about from the side of the house to the deeper shadows of yew trees that marked the edge of the property.

Making his way towards the back of the house, Monty waded through wild grasses that had sprung up, were brushing his legs and threatening to trip him. It was a small orchard of apple trees that brought him to a standstill. The tops of the trees were silhouetted against the folds of the hills and in the moonlight the trees wore their pruned wounds like military medals. Monty watched while images of his father and his father's father played beneath the branches. Once, no doubt, they had thrown small sticks into these trees to bring down the hanging fruit. Now, rotting apples fell by themselves and there was nobody to pick them up.

Beyond the trees and into the darkness, Monty made out the outbuildings that marked the boundary at the rear of the Villa Rosa. Nearing these old buildings, Monty discerned the split doors punched into a saggy and timbered construction. The doors suggested that these building had been stables. Perhaps, in the days of his grandfather, they had concealed an apple press. Next, it was the shadow of a hybrid vehicle - with caterpillar tracks at the back and a motorcycle wheel at the front - that caught his eye. The tyre at the front was flat and the handlebars had been thrown to one side as if the rider had recently jumped from the machine in order to look for a garage. This, Monty knew, was a military machine, half motorcycle and half tank, and produced during World War 2. In 2016, this *Kettenkrad* was a museum piece and part of Peter Lutz's collection.

A tap, tap, tapping from near at hand drew Monty back towards the main house. A door was swinging next to a shuttered window. Monty approached, put his hands on the window sill and peered through the shutters. The moon had made its way through and over the trees and in its light Monty saw music sheets strewn about the floor. It was the presence in the room of two people that grabbed for Monty's attention. Rows of Hitler heads stared across the room while the walls bore portraits of the man himself and of leading member of the Nazi Party, Hermann Goering. Monty thought the full-length portrait of Hitler on the wall to his left was particularly impressive because it reminded Monty just how much of the man's appeal was based on preening skills.

Monty felt a sense of the past here in the same way he had felt it on the battlefields of northern France. This house of ghosts made him shiver. It was a relic of his ancestors and nothing more nor less than the place from which all roads spread and to which all roads returned and gave substance to the saying that "the past beats inside us like a second heart."

By now, Monty was feeling like a thief intruding on someone else's life and passion. He stretched out his cheeks in a wide grimace. He had been making a habit of intrusion recently. It was most uncharacteristic of him. Three days previously he had been rifling through his own son's room and sneaking around in a most unforgivable manner. And yet, he had not dropped to the floor in a dead faint or worse. He was still here and now looking at the old stables and the trees in the secret garden. What was to prevent him from entering this house, too? What was more, who was going to stop him? There were no prefects, mouthing hugely, reminding him of what was right and what was wrong. There were no teachers around to remind him of his school motto. He was old enough to make his own decisions and, he reminded himself, desperate times needed desperate measures.

Monty stepped away from the window and pushed at the door. It swung open.

There was a tap on his shoulder and a hiss in his ear.

"What's all this? What on earth are you doing here?"

16

Saturday – early evening

Monty swung round. Careful to keep his weight on his back foot, he raised both arms to protect his head in the way he had been taught in boxing lessons at school. At the same time, his heart jumped first against his sternum and then beat in his neck like running feet. He breathed out:

"Jesus..."

He wanted to say more but he was now a little breathless.

Nothing to worry about, Monty. Just relax and it will go away. At least there's no chest pain, no dizziness.

But there was that pregnant pause, the long build-up to the thump and that pitter-patter in his neck.

You should see a doctor, Monty.

He really did not want to waste his doctor's time. He was a busy man who had little time for hypochondriacs. Controlling his breathing, keeping his voice down and monitoring that heartbeat, Monty said:

"For God's sake, do you have to creep up on people like that?"

"I've been keeping an eye on you, dad. I know why you are here."

Julian was looking over Monty's right shoulder. Maybe he had seen someone walking through the darkness towards them - Peter Lutz perhaps. Monty had a need to turn around and look for himself but he kept his eyes fixed on Julian's. This was no easy task. The boy was agitated and said into the dark spaces behind Monty's back:

"Dad, the man's just not... He's a complete nutter - a maniac. He's capable of anything. He thinks he can save the German people by carrying on the work started by his father. He thinks he's..."

He then clammed up as though he had been speaking to an apparition which had suddenly melted into the night.

"I'll be fine," Monty said.

He felt anything but "fine." Not only would his heart refuse to beat normally, he felt uncomfortable at Julian's expression of concern and a need to interrupt the emotions that were flying between them.

"Quick, go now," Monty said.

He extended his arm with the intention of pushing his son away but when his arm was at full stretch, Julian put out his own hand and his fingertips briefly brushed Monty's. In that slightest of contact, there was a tremor, a shift in their relationship, a glimpse into what Julian had been trying to say to him and into what Monty had been longing to hear. Then, awkwardness returned along with its stiffness, formality and regrets.

"Take this," Julian said, pushing a small torch into Monty's hand. "It's dark in there. He already put me in the coal room for threatening to go to the police. He's a psychopath, he..."

But Monty was not listening.

"I'll be fine. Now, just go home, Julian."

Regretting the sharp tone of his voice, he added:

"If I'm not home within two hours, ring the police, just in case..."

Julian nodded.

"I'll do that, dad."

Monty watched his son turn and walk away and wondered how he was able to reject him and let him go without another touch, a kiss or a hug. He watched until Julian's shape in the darkness became merely a crunch of shoes on the gravel and until, in the end, the two of them were bound together by silence.

Sliding the torch into the pocket of his leather jacket, Monty sauntered off across the no-man's-land between the house and the stables wondering why he had been so curt. He remembered the letter in his back pocket and felt regret at the dismissive tone of his voice. Perhaps it was not Julian he was rejecting. An idea came to him, a fleeting thought, no more than a gust of wind, that it was feelings about his own father he was afraid of.

Passing the hybrid vehicle, Monty suppressed the ridiculous idea that its rider had only recently dismounted and would be back any second. There would be no returnings or second comings and there would be no second chances. Perhaps he should compose a letter of his own. He had phrases of apology already made in his head. *Sorry I have not been the perfect father you wanted. I am sorry you feel you can't communicate with me. I regret not giving you more support when you needed it. I regret not being able to express my love. I regret leaving it all unsaid.*

Arriving at the double doors of the main stable, Monty had dismissed the idea of a written apology. The notion that he should express regret for not showing enough love was simply pathetic. It was what he did now that was important. Perhaps, Monty thought, he should simply be more attentive and things would clear up of their own accord.

When Monty pulled at the stable doors and fumbled for the light switch, he was not expecting any surprises. He had already seen a fraction of the collection of Nazi memorabilia and Lutz himself had told him that of all the military vehicles he owned most of them were housed in industrial buildings dotted around the county. Nor was Monty shocked by an interest and collection that were quite commonplace in England. The recent sale for $92000 of a rare German Enigma enciphering machine had even appeared as an item on the BBC news programme. However, Monty had lived long enough in Germany to know that attitudes there tended to be different. More importantly, so was the law. The German criminal code did not deal kindly with collectors of Nazi memorabilia and, in some circumstances, the collector faced a stiff fine and up to 3 years in prison. Monty's own view was that Peter's fascination was not so very different from a fascination with 1960s pop memorabilia or with *art deco* and its association with the Roaring Twenties and the depression.

But when the stable doors creaked open and the light of a solitary bulb flickered on, the need to empty his gut returned. The innumerable vehicle parts scattered over the floor conjured up visions of a motorway accident. But the aftermath of this tragedy was eerily quiet. There were no calls for help, no screams of men, women and children, no drivers running from burning cars and dodging the falling debris as if it were shrapnel. The only sound Monty heard came from the tall trees in the forest creaking in the wind.

Towering over the bits and pieces were wartime vehicles, now heaps of metal ravaged and worn by years spent in desert or steppe. Gun turrets lay amidst the wrecks of jeeps and motorbikes but everything was orderly as if the objects were queuing for something. The one complete tank - a grey-brown Panzer 1V - looked diseased beyond cure. It was patched with rust and scarred with bullet marks and its tracks were choked with shreds of barbed wire.

For Monty, every antique object, whatever era it came from, simply told its own unique story and it was a sense of this history that he felt now - a sense of the people who had fought in these vehicles, formed powerful friendships in them like that between his father and Ashley Mead. He could almost hear conversations recorded in the very presence of the objects themselves.

Glancing at his watch, Monty switched off the light, closed the double doors and swivelled away to find Lutz and confront him. Strolling back towards the house he reflected that a public exhibition of Lutz's artefacts would be against German law. What was more, many Germans would question whether the artefacts he had seen should be preserved at all. But Monty was not German, he was not unsympathetic to military collections and he thought he understood their fascination. As a boy, he had owned around 300 plastic soldiers and he had divided them up into regiments, each with its own quota of model tanks and guns. He would line them up in the garden and throw chunks of earth at them in mock-up battles of good versus evil. Perhaps it was this simplistic view of life and war that made these World War 2 objects so satisfying. Perhaps it was the very darkness of these museum pieces that attracted novelists, filmmakers, collectors and antique dealers like himself. Perhaps military memorabilia reminded these people just how good they really were.

When Monty arrived at the unlocked back door, he pushed it open and, with a glance at the moon, he stepped inside. The door closed with a light click and Monty turned sharply, his arms raised to defend himself.

Calm down, Monty, and stop being such an idiot.

How, he thought, could anyone mistake the click of a door for a cough or the scraping of a foot on concrete?

He ran a hand through his hair before resting both hands on his hips and taking in his surroundings. He found himself in a corridor that stretched out in front of him until blocked by the large wooden doorway through which he had passed with Lutz on his only other visit to the Villa Rosa. On his immediate left was the open door to the room he had seen from the garden - the Hitler room. Unzipping his leather jacket, Monty stepped forward.

In the Hitler room, the moonlight had faded to a single beam of light that shone on the floorboards and spread outwards to cover everything within reach in a veil of white. Amongst the busts and paintings of Nazi leaders were nails jutting out from the wall. The nails marked the spaces where other paintings had once been hanging, their presence celebrated by bleached squares framed by dust and dirt.

Monty left the room and felt his way along the poorly lit corridor, his fingertips brushing the woodwork until, just before the end of the corridor, a narrow flight of stairs led up through complete darkness to the ground floor. Cautiously, feeling the way with the tips of his feet and fingers, Monty climbed the stairs, the boards creaking under his weight. He paused on the ground floor to monitor his heartbeat. Satisfied that all was well, he continued up to an airy upper floor and another long corridor in which, Monty felt, he was reaching the heart of an obsession. The corridor was occupied by dozens of mannequins, all in Nazi uniform. Some were dressed as Hitler Youth, some as SS officers, others as *Wehrmacht* soldiers. It was quite still, the mannequins posing in ways that suggested they had frozen on the march, or were covered in ash like the bodies at Pompeii. One wall was lined with machine guns, rifles and rocket launchers while the opposite wall was blotched with photographs, military maps and sketches.

Monty gazed across this army of motionless Nazis, absorbed the uniforms, the bayonets, the glimmering guns while his blood sang in his ears to the irregular beat of his heart. He found that the air here was damp and cold enough to make him shiver and, on regaining his breath, he climbed another flight of stairs to find more pictures of Hitler on the walls, swastikas and iron crosses, and an oil portrait of Eva Braun. He picked his way between other artefacts, stepping over full and empty boxes. If Lutz did not curb his obsession, Monty thought, the collection would swallow up the entire house.

He passed along more unlit and shadowy corridors, through a door in a bookshelf and towards another winding staircase. Monty assumed that the moon was high above the house because he had no need of the torch Julian had given him. But he was comforted by the sight of stars through the windows and the sound of church bells reassured him by their normality. When the sound of the bells died away, the vagueness of a whistling wind seemed to fill the night.

The winding staircase was pitch black and Monty slipped the torch from his jacket pocket and flicked it on. He found himself in a cluster of rooms the size and shape of which suggested they had once been the servants' quarters. In the torchlight he made out cobwebs, broken pieces of furniture and more piles of uniforms. Monty was reaching into a wardrobe to pull out a white dress suit when he felt his heart thump again and the sensation brought a film of sweat to his brow. This particular thump was followed by a long pause while his heart seemed to skip a beat and balance on a knife edge while deciding whether to restart or not.

The intensity of the thump unsettled Monty. He had come to speak to Lutz, to confront him with his alleged wrongdoings. The feeling that he was now unwanted, an intruder in someone else's property welled up inside him.

Get out before you are found out, Monty.

He strode out of the room, clattered down the winding staircase, through the door in the bookcase and took the stairs down to the paintings and the mannequins two at a time. He hesitated, feeling his heart pound at a rapid pace. He checked his watch but the time did not register. He looked through the window, briefly noted that the trees were still swaying and the leaves were tumbling. On the ground floor, he congratulated himself that he had made it without being seen. Monty even allowed himself the luxury of a quiet word.

"Sad."

Monty heard a sound from the basement.

It was the same sound he had heard on entering the house – a cough or the scraping of a foot on the floor. He pushed through the door and crept down the steps and into the long corridor. The light from the rising moon had melted away but there was a new light, artificial light, emanating from under a door.

He stopped outside the room, knowing he should return home and rest. Instead, Monty put out his hand and pushed the door open. He stood still, catching his breath and then stepped through the doorway. Reaching for the zip of his jacket he fingered at it while passing the door to Hitler's cell in Landsberg. Stopping to listen, he pulled at the zip and stared at the rails of uniforms stretching away into the distance.

"So," said a voice, "I see you have let yourself in."

Monty stumbled backwards unsure whether or not he was losing his mind. The whole point of mannequins was they never moved. But one of the SS uniforms stepped forward, swivelled to face him and a voice said:

"No, you don't recognise me," said the voice. "No matter. I am sure that since you let yourself in, uninvited, so to speak, you don't mind being with me while I live out my fantasy."

17

Saturday – evening

It was the word "panther" that leaped into Monty's head - a vision of lithe blackness tipped with knee-length black boots and a black cap. The boots were polished and sparkled in the light.

"Magnificent, aren't they?" Lutz said. "A good fit, in fact. They need a lot of elbow grease to get them to shine like this."

Lutz stood about 10 metres away, his legs apart, his arms akimbo. His eyes were shadowed sockets under a black front peak adorned with eagle and skull.

"That's right – the boots used to belong to my father."

In many ways, Peter Lutz was the mystery neighbour. Monty knew Peter was often away. The empty house would bathe in perpetual darkness and the post-box would fill up with flyers until the weekly gardener arrived to cut the grass, sweep the leaves and remove all signs of absence - including the post. Peter's presence in the house was usually signalled by evening lights, the occasional sound of a slamming door and the beautiful

1970 Mercedes Pagoda in the drive. This meant that the memory of the man, a nervous individual with the quick movements of a blackbird and a penchant for English idiom, was more familiar to Monty than the real thing. The man was confusing Monty now because he seemed so relaxed, so self-confident and chatty.

"The boots would go for arms and legs these days," Peter said, "and so would the visor cap. Hard to get genuine ones; you know, the real McCoy."

Peter raised his right arm and scratched at the left collar of his jacket.

"The uniform is one my father would have worn. Yes, it's a 1936 general SS service dress uniform belonging to a S*turmbannfuehrer* – or major *auf Englisch, oder*?"

"Indeed, it is," Monty said.

Lutz slid his hand down across the black tie and back up to the collar.

"Yes, you know that was my father's rank, don't you? The four silver pips on the collar patch are the giveaway, aren't they?"

Lutz stretched out his cheeks in an imitation smile.

"An old dealer like you would want to know its value, wouldn't he?" Peter said. He pursed his lips and sucked in air with a prolonged hiss. "The whole kit and caboodle?"

While he made his estimate, there was no indication in his voice that he was challenging Monty to disagree. The tone suggested he and Monty understood each other.

"About 25000 dollars I would guess, perhaps more," Lutz said.

He cleared his throat while allowing his hand to slide from his shoulder, across the black diagonal shoulder strap and pleated black pockets to the black belt next to a black holster.

"Right again," Peter said. "Yes, you have it. In this

holster is my father's pistol. It's a Walther PPK as you know - very reliable and popular with the German military, the Police and the Luftwaffe. Did you know that Adolf killed himself with one in the *Fuehrer bunker* in 1945?"

Lutz puckered his lips and sucked at his cheeks. He then ran his tongue around the inside of his mouth. Monty followed the swelling shift from under his cheek, to the bottom lip and back up the other side of his face before it disappeared again. Lutz then fingered the holster and loosened the leather fastener.

"Look," he said, "my father's name is written on the inside flap. I find it all quite moving really. To touch with my fingers that which my father's fingers once touched - it gives me goose skin, you know."

Monty shivered. In the presence of the boots and the pistol he felt proximity not only to history but also to horror and that familiar feeling that the objects themselves knew more than they were telling. Lutz wrapped his hand around the butt of the pistol and drew it from the holster. He lifted it over his head and held it there as though it were a starting pistol.

"This one has not been fired for a long time. The shells are still inside. They are the ones my father would have loaded himself. So, I would like to keep things as they are. You understand me, don't you?"

Lutz nodded in a way that suggested he already knew the answer.

"Yes, you English do love your innuendo, don't you? I need to make sure I am not too oblique, you understand?"

Monty nodded along with Lutz. Peter eventually lowered his arm but he did not replace the pistol. He kept it hidden behind the pleats of his black jodhpurs.

"You know, Monty, I know what you are thinking," Lutz said.

Monty frowned. What he was thinking was hardly the issue. The issue, and the problem, was the gun and what Lutz might do with it. Lutz's behaviour frightened him. It was warped, as if the man had taken some kind of drug, something recreational like hashish or ecstasy. Monty opened his mouth to speak but before he could turn the topic of conversation to the purpose of his visit, Lutz broke into a bout of throat clearing and lip smacking. Eventually, he said:

"You think I am a Nazi, don't you? Umm? Am I right? Yes, I am right, aren't I? Yes, well you can think what you like. I usually try not to answer when people accuse me of being a Nazi. I tend to turn my back and leave them looking like silly billies. I think Hitler and Goering were such fascinating characters in so many ways. Hitler's eye for quality was second only to none."

The petulant tone of Lutz's voice concerned Monty. Petulance could often precede a change of mood. Monty stepped forward, affecting an interest in the uniforms brushing his shoulder. Every step brought him nearer to Lutz.

Just a precaution, Monty, but better safe than sorry.

He wanted to be closer to Lutz, to be able to tackle him should his mood change to something threatening. A movement of Lutz's arm stopped Monty in his tracks. Lutz had inserted a finger into the trigger guard and the pistol was dangling on it. Monty stopped in front of a mannequin and examined its uniform - that of a German tank commander.

"Actually," he said, "I have never thought of you as a Nazi."

"No?"

"No."

Monty shoved his hands into the back pockets of his jeans. The feeling of the letter against his fingers brought him back to himself. It somehow reassured him that part of his son was with him.

"You really take me for a fool, don't you?" Lutz said. "But don't worry, I won't take it personally and anyway the safety catch is on."

"What I think," Monty said, "is that you are a collector of military artefacts, nothing more or less."

Lutz considered for a moment and Monty took the opportunity to jump in with a joke to lighten the atmosphere.

"I am a dealer in lost property," he said, "but that doesn't mean that I, too, am an item of lost property, does it?"

But Monty was disturbed to see that Lutz had not heard him. He had disappeared into a world of his own.

"Nothing more or less? You have seen what there is outside. That half-track was designed by the Nazis to say 'Up yours, Jack' to the terms of the Versailles treaty. I own more of them than anyone else in the world. Some I picked up for around $1,500. I can sell them for over $200,000. But they just look very cool," he added with a grin. "The Panzer 1V you saw in the stable cost me $20,000 but I was once offered considerably more for it."

He studied Monty for several seconds, watching the effect of his words.

"Yes, yes," he said, "it all adds up to millions. Millions. And I know what you are thinking. You are thinking that I inherited a fortune from my father, that I'm a spoilt rich kid who wants to indulge in these toys."

For the first time there was a defensive edge to his voice.

"It's not like that at all. My dad supported me, yes. But only when I could prove that the collection would work financially. And as a collector, you never have any spare money lying around. Everything is tied up in the collection."

He seemed to be making some sort of confession but, Monty thought, confessions were not usually made by men holding pistols and Lutz was spinning his pistol on one finger.

"But I have not collected all this for the money. It is the link to the past. It's a very special feeling. And I want people to see this stuff. There's no better way to understand history. I want to preserve things. I want to show the next generation how it actually was. And this collection is a kind of memorial to those who didn't come back."

The pistol was still spinning. After two or three rotations Lutz would catch the butt and send it spinning again in the opposite direction.

"You know, you did just make me think," he said.

"About?"

"About the point of owning these things if nobody's ever going to see them."

"You can..."

But Lutz was now looking over Monty's head and towards the door. Either, Monty thought, there was someone at the door or Lutz was conversing with voices inside his head.

"The Germans? No, they don't give two monkeys about this stuff. Many of them act as if history never happened. Public display? Out of the question. It would land me in prison."

Lutz was already breathing hard. He had been getting more and more upset as he spoke and the pistol was spinning faster as it caught the urgency of his voice. Now, he broke into another fit of coughing. When the fit had passed, he seemed tired and depressed.

"I've spent, I suppose, 40 years as a collector, just plodding along, and I've suddenly realized that there's more time behind than ahead. I need to do something

146

important with my life - something that would have made my father proud."

Monty touched his hair with his fingertips, took a deep breath and exhaled quickly, eager to move on.

"Important?" Monty said with a smile.

Lutz spread his arms out in such a sudden and violent movement that his pistol struck an unfortunate mannequin on the chin. Lutz merely glanced sideways and took two steps forward, his gun now raised slightly to the left of Monty's shoulder.

"Yes, important things, things which require more money than I have at beck and call at the moment. But in order to be a big cheese, and in order to make my father proud, I will have to think from out of the box, like he did."

"So - for example?"

"Oh, come on, Monty. You can guess, can't you? The market is flat but the collection is insured for a fortune. Maybe it will go up in flames."

Lutz moved a little closer to Monty in a manner that suggested he would speak into his ear.

"You can see the scenario, can't you? Of course, you can. A burglar comes - a clumsy oaf like you - he starts a fire and the whole lot goes up. Imagine such a thing."

"There are no burglars here," Monty said.

"Oh, come on, Monty. Don't play the feather brain with me. Use your head. Imagine the scene: the burglar, the matches and the petrol, eh? Think about it..."

Monty did just that and he felt his heart thump and then pause on a knife edge in his neck.

18

"Don't look so worried," Lutz said. "It was just a joke. I thought you English liked jokes."

Monty decided to call Lutz's bluff.

"Alright," he said. "If you need the money, burn the whole collection. Why don't you?"

"It had never seriously crossed my mind."

Monty was not entirely convinced about this claim. There had been a look in Lutz's eye that suggested he had unwrapped the idea in order to consider it, test reactions to it like a man trialling a new product - perfume perhaps - on shoppers in a busy street.

"Perhaps," Monty said, "it was just a passing thought?"

Lutz became suddenly serious.

"Burn my father's house? His uniform and..."

He indicated the rows of mannequins and added:

"Burn my father's personal bodyguard? You are pulling my legs, aren't you? Tell me you are pulling my legs."

"Maybe just one leg," Monty said.

Peter bent at the waist as though he had been punched. His laugh began in his stomach, continued as a series snorts and ended in a long wheeze. He straightened up and shook his head.

"You English and your jokes."

"So," Monty said. "You were saying. These important things you mentioned, things that will make your father proud. Can you be more specific?"

Lutz seemed to find his question amusing. His wheezing, which had not stopped, now developed into a lighter laugh. It was not a belly laugh and it was not a chuckle. "Snigger" was the best word that came to Monty's mind, and its associations with mischief or lies.

"I will achieve something - make a difference before I go west. You know how it is at our age, this feeling of regret at lost opportunities, am I right?"

Monty made a non-committal wag of his head. He was reluctant to agree with this man but he was right. Monty had to admit that, at around sixty, regrets popped up and clamoured for his attention: regret at time wasted worrying what others thought about him, regret at not achieving anything of note, regret at not letting Julian become what he wanted to be and regret at not realising sooner that love, compassion and empathy were more important than discipline. Just recently he had glimpsed another regret coming down the track - regret at not having the confidence to trust his own thoughts and feelings and expressing them. Yes, Lutz was right but Julian was right, too. His assessment of Lutz was not far from the truth. The man was a maniac and needed help.

"I don't know about you," Lutz said, apparently reading Monty's thoughts, "but I'm learning to help myself. Nobody else will. I am already working on it. The process of change is under way."

"Already?"

Lutz hooked the thumb of his free hand in the black

trouser belt, threw one leg forward and rested his weight on his back foot. His head was cocked and he looked at Monty in amusement.

"Yes, you have to grab the bull by the horn when the opportunity comes along."

"To which horn are you referring?"

"The refugees, of course. Such opportunities, don't you think?"

Monty scratched the back of his head. He had read the arguments in favour of accepting large numbers of refugees. It was an opportunity not to be missed. Germany was, after all, facing a future of an aging and declining population. Many migrants came with the skills and motivation to boost the workforce with numbers, new ideas and fresh perspectives. But Monty guessed that Lutz's was not referring to opportunities concerning the integration of refugees.

"Opportunities for whom?" Monty said.

"Opportunities for me, of course. Opportunities to make something of myself and to become someone Germany and my father can be proud of. You know, Monty, one of the great skills in life is to recognise an opportunity when it comes. And when it comes you must take it with both hands. *Man muss das Eisen schmieden, solange es heiss ist.* How do you say that in English?"

"Strike while the iron is hot," Monty said.

"Exactly. Strike while the iron is hot. That's good. I like that."

"And what, exactly, is of such burning importance?" Monty asked.

He had been attempting another joke in order to lighten up the situation. Lutz still had his thumb in the trouser belt but the other hand was used for frightening gestures, the arm rising with the word "strike" and crashing down on the word "hot." It was not the similarity to Hitler's body language that kept Monty's heartbeat on a knife edge, but the pistol swivelling on the end of Lutz's index finger.

Lutz composed himself, looked down at the floor and then up at Monty in the manner of a bashful boy who knew he had overstepped the mark. He said:

"There is a feeling amongst many Germans."

"Which is?"

"That we are not allowed to express things because of our Nazi past. But I am giving the people the possibility."

"To do...?"

"To say what they want and express what they feel."

"And do you know what they want?"

Lutz raised his head.

"They have a desire for tighter immigration controls, for keeping war refugees in their homelands, for forcing foreigners in Germany to speak German at home and for the swifter deportation of asylum seekers who do not respect our laws and norms."

"Like those who apparently attack women in the street?"

"Exactly. Whenever it happens, the fears of the people, the fears of refugee helpers; the fears of unknown women and the fears of Chancellor Angela Merkel come true. But I will give the people a voice."

"I see. And how and when do you intend to do that?"

Monty asked the question as calmly as he could but the pistol was spinning again. First in one direction and then the other, its movement was irregular and utterly unpredictable.

"It is not a question of how or when," Lutz said. "The process is under way - as I told you. I am the *Sturmbannfuehrer*. You know that, right?"

Lutz engaged with Monty's eyes.

"Yes, of course you do. So, you know about the *Vaterlaendische Front*, don't you?"

He did not wait for Monty to respond. The pistol span faster and faster now, his words ran in response to it and his eyes opened up like moons.

"Have you any idea how many we are now? In just a few months we have achieved a following of many thousands. And we all have common aims. Do you want to know what these aims are? To maintain our culture, our language and our heritage and to rid this country of Ali Baba and his forty drug dealers."

Peter paused to catch his breath and Monty jumped in with a question he had often discussed with Ingrid.

"You don't think they will integrate and become a part of Germany?"

Lutz clenched the butt of the pistol but sent it spinning again when he spoke.

"If you think that, you are either living in cloud cuckoo land or you're a fool. The number of refugees is terrifying. Don't forget that we are an aging population. The refugees could push us towards a future in which half the under forty population in Germany would consist of Middle Eastern and North African immigrants and their children. Do you really think that German society is likely to peacefully absorb a migration of that size and scale of cultural difference?"

His voice stopped as abruptly as the spinning of the pistol in his hand. It was clear to Monty that Lutz had thought about the topic on many occasions. Lutz now grabbed the butt in the palm of his hand and then pointed the weapon at Monty.

"If you do then you are up a gum tree, my friend."

"So, what do we do?" Monty asked. "Do we allow them to drown in droves in the Mediterranean?"

Monty's sarcastic tone resulted in a hint of irritation appearing in Lutz's eyes. He responded by assuming a university lecturer's stance, leaning forward and using the pistol as a pointer.

"Such a transformation of German society will lead to increasing polarization among natives and new arrivals alike. It threatens not just a spike in terrorism but a rebirth of 1930s-style political violence."

With one eye on the pistol, Monty tried to calm the man down or at least to bring him to a reasonable level of stability.

"Let us hope that neither of us lives in cloud cuckoo land," he said.

But Lutz seemed to interpret Monty's concern with the gun for inattentiveness and dealt with it by raising his voice.

"It need not happen. Common sense dictates. We must stop this madness. We must close the border. We must send them back. We must stop trying to atone for our past with this reckless humanitarianism in the here and now."

Lutz stopped to breathe and, despite the gun, Monty could not stop himself from provoking Lutz with:

"No doubt, at the same time, you will expand the *Vaterlaendische Front* into a political force to be respected."

"Of course."

"I'm sure the people - and your father - would be proud of you."

Monty's sarcastic tone was lost on Lutz. Instead he seemed to melt, seemed vulnerable while the barrel of the pistol tilted towards the ground. At this time of weakness, Monty decided it was his turn to attack.

"Tell me, please, about my son. Julian was a willing recruit for you, was he?"

Monty flinched. He had not intended to formulate his question like that but there it was, hovering in the air between them.

"So - that is why you have come? Perhaps he has come to you and spoken about the pickle he is in. Am I right?"

Monty ignored the question's tone and the accompanying chuckle and waited a moment before saying:

"I am his father."

Lutz almost lunged at Monty, his arms and the gun waving in the air.

"Yes, you are his father - but in name only. And you are a fool. No fool like an old fool, eh, Monty? But what do you know about your son? Do you know what his hobbies are? Do you know what music he likes? Do you know which drugs he takes? What do you know about his sexual preferences and when did you last tell him that you love him?"

Monty allowed this barrage to pass him - a gust of wind that barely ruffled his big hair and clothes. But try as he might, Monty could not recall the last time he had told Julian that he loved him. It was a hard thing to say. Until his son was around 16 years old Monty had adopted his own father's paternal style because there had been no other role model. And like his father, Monty saw his role as that of a fair disciplinarian. He tried to teach Julian what his own father had taught him. Crime was met with punishment, poor manners were countered with condemnation, and rudeness with a disciplinary action of which his old school and his own father would have been proud. This was not a role that required declarations of love.

Monty thought that the opportunity to change things was hidden in the back pocket of his jeans. Julian's letter came in the aftermath of Friday evening's heated exchange in the fish bowl room. The content of the letter was cruel. It was the end result of his failure to be a good father, years of opportunity squandered because he had never had enough time. The only positive thing he could take from the letter was that Julian had cared enough to write it. It was now Monty's turn to show he cared enough to reciprocate.

"You know, Monty, Julian and people like him are just perfect for my purposes."

"What do you mean 'people like him'?"

Lutz pursed his lips and blew slowly through them. Eventually, and in a tone, which suggested he had settled for second best, he said:

"I mean, lost boys. Boys with no emotional roots. Boys who..."

Monty refused to hear more. He raised both arms and held his hands up and palm outwards as if intent on keeping Lutz's words at bay. Mistaking Lutz's open mouth for a sign of surprise, Monty said roughly:

"Boys who what? And what is your purpose?"

Lutz raised the gun. It and his hands were shaking in time to his uneven whisper.

"Do not interrupt me when I am talking. Do not use that tone to me. I am the *Sturmbannfuehrer*, and don't forget it."

While Lutz was making an effort to control himself, Monty saw the developing picture of the individual in front of him. Like the building of an internet page, the complete picture emerged - banner by banner and headline by headline. The finished product had a headline all to itself. It read: Peter Lutz is seriously disturbed.

"These lost boys can help me to further my aims," he said. "You recruit those who are vulnerable - those with something to hide. You groom them. Groom is the right word, isn't it?"

Monty nodded but Lutz made no comment and gave no sign that he had seen Monty's nod, no sign that he was going to place the gun in its holster.

"You get to know these people, befriend them and when you have a new friend you ask them to help you, put them under pressure. You can even use blackmail."

Monty kept his eyes on the pistol, smiled and said nothing.

"You know, Monty, for years I have had dealings with this gang of motorbike riders - a sort of Hells Angels chapter - at least that is how they see themselves. Some of them have bought small items of memorabilia from me. Others deal in drugs. One of them has a prime spot near the university where Julian studies. What a coincidence that is."

Lutz stretched his cheeks to imitate a smile but his eyes were dancing a fast waltz as they looked around the room.

"Don't stop there," Monty said.

"Julian was a user, a heavy user. I don't suppose a man like you would know but it is easy for a user to become a pusher. Julian was associated with drugs. People came to him and asked him to find drugs for them. This is how it works, you know? Julian needed money to support his habit so he went back to his supplier and asked for more drugs at a discounted price. You don't need a university degree to see the financial benefits for your son, do you, Monty? Clearly, he's a chip off the block. You should be proud of him."

Monty surprised himself at how easy it was to ignore these jibes.

"Old block," he said. "A chip off the old block. Don't forget the word 'old,' OK?"

Monty clenched his fists and waited for the storm he felt was coming. Instead, there was a long moment of calm while Lutz considered Monty's comments. Eventually, he made a dipping movement of the head and lightly clicked the heels of his black boots.

"Thank you so much for your correction," he said. "Any other corrections would be greatly appreciated. My English will be perfect. Perfect. Anything else simply will not do."

His gaze danced round the room again before coming to rest on the mannequins beside him.

"Conversation with these stiffs can be a bit limiting."

Monty managed a smile and nodded.

"So, let me understand. You find vulnerable people, you offer them help and then you blackmail them, am I right?"

"Exactly. You have them over the barrel, as you English like to say. Is that the correct expression?"

"Indeed, it is," Monty lied. "Perfect. Just perfect."

"So," Lutz went on. "You ask them to do things for you. You start slowly, you ask them for favours. And it is difficult to refuse when you have a gang of thugs breathing down your neck. My motorcycle boys have been most useful. But little reminders here and there..."

He seemed to like the sound of the words "here and there." He swayed sideways to the rhythm of his words and held the pistol as if it were a microphone.

"The penalty for selling drugs is very harsh in Germany," Lutz said. "Between one and fifteen years, you know? People will do a lot to avoid such a sentence - even join the *Vaterlaendische Front*. In Julian's case, we had something else on him."

"Please take the gun away from your mouth," Monty said.

"He is, shall we say, sexually ambiguous."

Lutz paused and waited for his words to sink in. Then he started giggling.

"Yes, that's right. Gay, a bum bandit, queer..."

The giggling was mild at first but it gradually got out of control until he was bending forward at the waist and snorting again. Eventually, wheezing heavily, he stood upright.

"You English," he said. "You have such expressive words for this sort of illness."

157

Monty watched him. He supposed he should have been angry or irritated but neither of these adjectives described his mood. But if Lutz allowed his finger to slip and blew his own head off, Monty saw himself simply turning around and walking away.

"So, you were blackmailing him?" Monty said.

"Such an ugly word 'blackmail,' don't you think?"

"Yes, it comes from..."

"I don't care where it comes from," Lutz snapped. "And I don't care for you blaming me. Julian's father has a lot to answer for. Not the most tolerant of men, I hear. He is merely someone who pays the university fees and bills but who cannot suffer those filthy gays at any price. I believe Julian wants to come to his father for help but doesn't have the courage to do so. I can't say I blame him. Tough situation, eh, having an old fart for a father? Someone should shoot the bastard."

There was nothing in Lutz's face to suggest he had attempted a joke. His expression was impassive and the gun was now pointing in Monty's direction.

"Very kind," Monty said. "Thanks."

"There's no need to thank me," Lutz said. "Just take a good look at yourself. Know what you'd see? A man who spies on his son. Terrible thing to do, don't you think? Imagine spying on your own son. And we thought it only happened in Nazi Germany and the DDR. What do you make of a father who spies on his son, Monty? What do you think the man's wife would do if she found out?"

At the sight of Lutz's grinning face, Monty felt the first stirrings of fear. He told himself not to react, not to engage with his interrogator. He shook his head and tutted.

"A shocking state of affairs," he said.

"You know, Monty, the same man searched his son's room. His son knew it was his father. He even knew which packets of drugs this idiotic man had opened. Of course, he told me immediately."

Monty made a quick calculation. "Immediately" must have been the day before when Julian had come home. "Immediately" must have been after he had left the house to meet his friends in the bar.

"So, you mean yesterday evening," Monty said.

Lutz nodded.

"And how did he do that?"

"He came to see me - during the celebrations. It was only the second time we had met face to face. Until then we had communicated online and through the Angels..."

"Yesterday? You met yesterday?"

"That is correct. And he came to see me this morning, too. The poor boy is in deep trouble. Perhaps he has told you. He wanted out. I had to put him in solitary, just to cool off. I don't like turncoats. I was forced to remind Julian that I have everything stored on my hard drive up the stairs."

"Everything?"

"Yes. Everything. That means everything from our first contact through to photographs taken during the operation last Wednesday. I am sure the police would love to know who threw that bomb, wouldn't they?"

Monty barely felt the anger tugging at the muscles of his face but he heard it in a word he muttered under his breath now. It was a word he had not used for years and he even managed to say it with a smile on his face.

"You fucker."

He was not entirely sure whether he was talking to himself or to Lutz. Monty was ashamed and afraid. He had failed as a father when Julian had come to him for help. It was only yesterday that he had opened his heart. Monty had doubted him then. He was still doubting him when he heard himself say:

"Julian threw the bomb? No, it could not have been

159

Julian. I just don't believe it."

"Well, the photographs tell another story. I was there, too, you know, robed and hooded. I got him to hold the device and took photographs of the man holding the flaming torch."

Lutz was staring intently into Monty's face. For a moment Monty was paralysed by fear - fear of his only child imprisoned for murder. He had no alternative but to clench his jaw, focus on Lutz's face and say:

"But he didn't throw it, did he?"

Monty waited, beads of sweat rising on the skin of his chest and pausing in their tracks. Time was Russian roulette and any click could change his life forever - click, click, click.

"No, he couldn't do it. I tried everything. I told him I would betray his drug dealing to the police but not even the threat of a prison sentence could change his mind. Not even the threat of telling his stupid father that his son is a queer could move him. I took the flaming bottle from him and threw it myself. The problem is that I was careless. The hood must have slipped and I think he recognised me."

Monty quivered and a bead of sweat rose and ran down his chest. Free from tension, Monty stumbled forward as though released from a force that had bound him to the floor.

"Stop where you are."

Lutz had raised the pistol and it was pointing at Monty's head.

Careful, Monty. This man has already burned one man alive. He won't hesitate to kill you.

"But I think," Lutz said, "I have told you far too much already. It must be the drugs. They make you so loquacious."

He reached over to a chair and picked up its cushion. Holding the cushion at waist height he shoved the barrel into it.

Monty closed his eyes and waited for the bullet to hit. His father had once told him what it felt like to be hit by a bullet. It hit you before you even heard the gun fire. Monty waited for the numbness. He waited for the excruciating burning sensation. Would he live or would he die? The human body was riddled with vital arterial thoroughfares. If one of these got punctured it could be lethal. His father had told him that with bullets, it all came down to placement and passage. That meant life or death depended on nothing more than luck.

Instead of numbness and pain, there was a voice.

"No, not now. I have a much better idea."

It was Lutz's voice.

"I shall tell you later what it is. Now, come with me. Like father, like son, Monty. You simply must cool off."

19

Saturday night/Sunday morning

Monty could not say how long he had been in the room when he first heard noises by the door. He had been drifting with his thoughts and so happy to be alive that he disallowed distractions from without. The room's dimensions - no more than 3 by 3 metres - did not worry or frighten him. The fact that he was locked in, imprisoned in this bunker was irrelevant. The aftershocks of his near-death experience were still present in his shivering body and his trembling hands. He hardly noticed the three black-streaked walls and merely noted with interest the fourth wall but let his fancy fly away with it as it sloped up to a bricked-up coal hole. Coal holes, he knew, were usually located in an outside wall near the street allowing the easy delivery of coal, generally in sacks and usually from horse-drawn carts. The smell of coal was not the only residue of this bygone period. Black dust, a few lumps of the coal itself and a few wood shavings had been swept up and piled high in one corner of the bunker.

Little things brought Monty happiness. At least Lutz

had left the light on - a single bulb burning from a socket in the wall. And he had a chair to sit on from which he eyed the rows of empty bottles, the piles of cloth and the Jerry cans by the wall. He had already examined them. They were 5-gallon cans, all of them were full of petrol and each weighed about 20 kilos. They were red and relatively new and would not be part of Lutz's military collection. Monty had to remind himself that it was oil and not petrol that might be used for a house's heating system and he had seen no petrol-burning garden vehicles. He could not think why anyone would keep cans of petrol hidden in a cellar. Worse, there was a small book of matches on the floor. *This stuff should really be in the garage*, he thought but then he remembered another garage, another box of matches and another time, many years ago, and the irresistible temptation these cans and matches had been to those two boys named Monty and Paul.

He mused on the ridiculousness of his position. Not so long ago a Wimbledon Grammar School for Boys reunion had given him the opportunity to compare himself with his contemporaries and see for himself how he was doing in life. The reunion had offered a chance to catch up, laugh, drink, share stories about the old days and assess the changes in others and compare them to his. Monty had enjoyed every moment of the reunion but when it was over, he said to himself: I have no regrets. I have done a good job with my life - a very good job.

He looked around the coal bunker he occupied and smiled a warped smile. One moment he was a respected dealer in lost property, the next moment he was a prisoner in a coal bunker. How random life was. How quickly lives could change - for everyone. Change came from the unexpected diagnosis, the phone call from the police, the madman with an automatic rifle, the envelope propped up against the breakfast marmalade containing a note from a never-to-return partner. You were going to die, your wife had had an accident, your husband or wife was leaving you. Lives could change in a moment. But sometimes, Monty thought, you lived for years without noticing anything while the problems smouldered. One day - whoosh - it went up in your face.

Monty slid his hand into his back pocket and drew out Julian's letter. The problem with Julian, for example, had been lying dormant for years but Monty had not seen it coming. He had not even received that call from the police telling him his son was dealing in drugs or suspected of murder. Nonetheless he had been obliged to do the unthinkable. He had broken two of his long-held values - do not disturb the privacy of others and do not spy or sneak on them. The memory of himself, searching the drawers and cupboards in Julian's room, shamed him. It was mortifying to recall that he had looked for depravity on Julian's computer, read his emails and examined websites visited.

Monty looked up. He thought he had heard a sound coming from outside the door. He was tempted to get up, walk to the door and demand if someone was there. He listened again. It was a scratching sound - perhaps mice or rats looking for scraps. Monty shook himself. He was safe where he was for the moment. His quivering body and trembling hands had now confined themselves to an occasional twitch or spasm but Monty felt mentally strong enough to send out his mind and reflect on his conversation with Lutz. Recreating the scene in his mind's eye, Monty thought he had performed well, remained stoic in the face of provocation and demonstrated admirable restraint in dealing with Lutz's attempts to humiliate him. Like many of his values, stoicism and restraint were qualities for which he had Wimbledon County Grammar to thank.

When Monty was around 14 years old, a school fellow named Bill Raisin, whose father was a member of Wimbledon Conservative Party, made Monty's life a misery by claiming Monty was a rotten German. At first, Monty rubbished these allegations. Of course, he was English. He had been born there and spoke English as a first language. Essentially, he was as English as roast beef and Yorkshire pudding. But the name, Brodnitz, was glaring. This meant that Bill held Monty responsible for the bombs that had fallen on the borough of Wimbledon during the blitz, the houses the bombs had destroyed, and the one that had taken out Centre Court in October 1940. When Monty refused to respond to these taunts, his tormentor went up a gear and called Monty a Jew killer and a loser.

At first Bill restricted his behaviour to verbal taunts and abuse, but the quieter Monty became, the more physical was the bullying. His exercise books were torn up, his cap dropped down the toilet, and ink was spilled over his text books.

The school code encouraged boys to sort out problems such as these on their own initiative and Monty did just that. Because Bill claimed to be the ringleader of a rough Wimbledon gang, Monty ruled out the use of fisticuffs. He therefore decided on other tactics. When his tormentor tried to parody a German accent, Monty laughed and Bill Raisin backed off. Monty then reversed the power roles by questioning his tormentor, trying to get inside his head and to understand his need to bully. Much to Monty's relief, his strategy worked. It emerged that Bill's father was a violent man, who would pick on his children when he was drunk - which was often. Twenty years later, Bill Raisin contacted Monty to ask for forgiveness. Actually, Monty had forgiven the boy years previously but he agreed to meet the man and listen to his apology.

There was another sound. It was louder this time, too loud for mice or rats. Monty folded the letter he was still holding, and slid it back into his pocket. The door shook, became still and then shook again. Someone was trying to get in. There was a metallic click and the door flew open and crashed against the wall. There was a voice.

"I thought he might put you in the coal room."

It was the click of the door latch that brought Monty back to the world. It was like a military command or the "get set" at school sports days. The first thing Monty was aware of was Julian. While he looked into Julian's face, the reality of their plight came back to him. Lutz had evidence against Julian that might send him to jail for a long time. There was only one course of action open to them: get Lutz's electronic devices and wipe their memories. All this came to Monty in an instant. Without saying a word, he reached for a bottle, removed its stopper and grabbed the nearest jerry can.

20

Sunday – early morning

Monty considered himself to be a careful and tidy man but there was no time to bother about the petrol cascading down from the lip of the bottle and flooding over the floor. Speed was the answer, keeping one move ahead of the words running through his head. *Don't do this, Monty. You'll end up in jail.* But he refused to listen. Instead, he found a joyous freedom in swinging the jerry can back and forth and not giving a damn whether the petrol ended up over the floor, the walls or the ceiling. Julian followed his father as if he was Monty's shadow but Monty elbowed him aside, and threw the half-empty can to the floor. Monty knelt and soaked a piece of cloth in the liquid glugging from its neck.

"Dad, dad, wake up. We've got to get out of here. What the hell are you doing? Stop this..."

Monty half-turned, stood up and shouldered Julian and his interruptions aside while stuffing the cloth into the neck of the bottle. There was no time to think, no time to reflect that he had acted like this in a garage with

Paul when he was a child. Monty was mouthing three words running like a news ticker through his head. Those words, taken from one of Julian's websites, on how to make a Molotov cocktail, had somehow imprinted themselves on Monty's brain - perhaps because Monty liked the voiced plosive sounds /d/, /p/ of the words "dispersed," "petrol" and "droplets."

He bent forward and picked up the book of matches. He lit the wick, pulled back his arm and hurled the flaming-wicked bottle to the floor. Both he and Julian threw themselves sideways when the bottle smashed on impact. Clouds of petrol droplets and vapour ignited and caused an immediate fireball followed by a spreading flame.

There was a rush of heat, the crackling of flames and a bang as the solitary bulb in the wall socket burst. The remaining content of the petrol can was a roaring flame that touched the ceiling. A sharp pain on his knuckle made Monty cry out and snatch his hand away. The cry acted as a starting pistol that sent him and Julian racing through the door and into the cellar corridor. Monty half-turned, looked back through the flickering yellow light, and hesitated as though considering a replay. But it was too late to dash back and repair things. The opportunity had passed him by in the flicker of an eye. The way back was obscured by a crackling flame and thick black smoke. This was not like the smoke he had seen in films or in his dreams. He did not imagine himself or Julian clamping damp rags over their mouths and battling through the thick black stuff rolling along the corridor behind them.

They broke through into a large space and, in the yellow light, Monty got a sense of where he was. To his right were the SS uniforms, rail after rail of them lined up as if on parade. To his left were the mortars, the shells, the enigma machines and the searchlights. There was a shout in his ear.

"Quick, dad, we can't stop here. Look."

He indicated the smoke. It was catching up with them, turning the black uniforms of the mannequins into a faded grey. A popping sound from behind made Monty turn. The SS man nearest the coal hole had lost his head in the heat and his uniform was smouldering. Monty almost expected to see him take swipes at himself to brush away the flames from his clothes, hear his scream and the prolonged moans of a man in his death throes. It would have been no surprise to see the dying man's comrades running behind him and escaping with their lives. But the figures were motionless, apparently intent on holding their positions and resisting to the end - a useless last stand against an overpowering enemy. Some of the mannequins were already falling, their faces sizzling and twisted, their heads popping, the fabric of their uniforms scorching and flaming. As the smoke began to flood into the open space, towards the door and the stairwell, Monty saw some faces crack. They resembled overcooked joints of meat, their cheeks running with fat.

My God, Monty, what have you done?

The light was brighter now, yellow and red and flickering and the smell was making Monty gag. He reeled away towards safety lurching first into a wall and then into mannequins. Many of them had lost the battle - their arms and legs losing tension before the models dropped to the floor.

Monty cupped his mouth but something stung his cheek. He brushed away a piece of smouldering ash. The area was full of ash and there were burning scraps of paper floating through the air and glimmering like May bugs. Monty squinted against the heat and raised his arm. These were the seconds that Monty later replayed in his mind - those seconds of horror when faced with

169

the consequences of his actions. But there was no time to reflect. He and Julian had a couple of minutes before they passed out and died in the smoke. No sooner had he worked that out when there were shouts from upstairs, the sound of chair legs scraping. Monty tugged at Julian's elbow.

"We need to get out of here and up the stairs, destroy the records... Quick."

Monty put one leg in front of the other and staggered behind his son. His heart was thumping strangely in his chest and rebounding in his neck. He ignored it. He knew he should not ignore it. There was nothing else until, through this confusion of thought and feeling, this dash for survival, came a picture of Ingrid walking through the streets of Berlin. How was she getting on? He would ask her himself. He would survive. Julian would survive.

Julian was ducking forward but the back of his head seemed to be singed and smouldering, and Monty crashed up the stairs behind him and into the corridor with the smoke trailing behind them. There was a clatter of footsteps rushing down the stairs from the first floor and a tug at Monty's arm.

"This way."

Monty stumbled and staggered after his son. When Julian shot into the Hitler room, Monty fell head first through the door after him. He lay on his back drawing in huge gulps of air while his heartbeat lost its rhythm, balanced, flip-flopped. Monty tried to ignore the perspiration and the ache in his back and threw his head to one side to somehow escape from the smell. This was not a smell that carried him off to some comfortable place of childhood happiness. A campfire or a log fire at Christmas yuletide had nothing in common with this stench of burning wires, of smouldering carpets, curtains and uniforms, of cracking wall plaster or the toxic cloud of Peter Lutz's collection melting.

While he and Julian crouched down behind the door of the Hitler room, Monty saw the staring, bare-teeth scream face of Peter Lutz rushing past with two burly men in leather in pursuit. They were dragging a hose and grunting. Lutz was making high-pitched barking curses at the malfunctioning sprinkler system and screaming for the hose and for someone to throw the tap. Monty glanced sideways but Julian refused to meet his father's eyes. Lutz had once taken great pleasure in telling Monty and Julian about the pre-action fire sprinkler system that had been installed in his house. "Pre-action," Lutz said, "refers to the electronically operated valve that holds water from the pipes until needed. Valve operation is controlled by flame, heat or smoke detection, unless it has been deactivated."

"Did you deactivate it?" Monty asked.

Julian shrugged his shoulders and looked sheepish.

"Wasn't me," he said.

Before Monty could reply there was a splash and a roar from the basement.

"They got the hose on," Monty said. "You got a minute before they come back up. Go get the stuff now.... go, go, go."

As Julian dashed out, Monty fell sideways to the floor. There was a shuddering sound from the house that Monty assumed to be the water pressing against the plumbing. There were intermittent shouts and bumps from the basement suggesting that Lutz and his two men were having problems balancing the thrust of the water through the hose. Monty was dripping sweat and breathing heavily. He estimated that from the initial combustion to Julian's disappearance no more than 4 or 5 minutes had passed. It felt like hours of fear. Coughing and struggling for breath he buried his face in his forearm. There was a voice.

"We need to go. The water is back on."

It was Julian's voice and he was clasping the laptop and a mobile phone. At that moment a hissing sound and the showering of water told him that the sprinkler system had come on. As Julian helped Monty to his feet, he was suddenly airborne and Julian made towards the side door with Monty hanging over his shoulders. Monty heard a panic of voices coming up from the cellar, the whining of the fire alarm, and a glimpsed image of Lutz gasping for breath, crawling on all fours and gagging. Then, there was darkness.

21

Sunday – late afternoon

"Successful trip?" Ingrid said. "That's not for me to say. In fact, I was hoping that you could tell me."

She slipped into the car and pulled the door shut. Monty thought it better to remain silent and let his wife do all the talking. In this, the long-way-past-the-post-romantic era of their relationship, Monty was both aware and grateful that he was never able to take Ingrid at face value. Understanding her moods and emotions was a work in progress rather than advancement towards an end point when he could say, "At last, I understand her." Age also helped. Monty was long enough in the tooth to accept the fact that the right to be permanently happy was something you saw only in films and advertisements for beauty-enhancing products. For the rest of the world population, permanent happiness was a myth. On this day, the day of her return from Berlin, he was happy. He was also aware that Ingrid was out of sorts.

Monty had timed his arrival at the airport perfectly. No sooner had he pulled on the handbrake than he saw Ingrid wandering out into the glitter and lights of the arrival's hall. She was slipping her lipstick into her bag and her eyes were sliding from side to side in the manner of a person hounded by a stalker. Applying lipstick was something Ingrid rarely did. Now he came to think of it, Monty realised that she used makeup only when she was in need of a pick-me-up. What was more, that beloved link with her youth, her pony tail, looked listless and in need of a refreshing wash and dry. He reached for his mobile, scrolled his home number and pressed the dial button. There was a click and Julian's voice crackled in Monty's ear.

"That you, mum?"

Monty stumbled over his next words. The word "dad" did not come easily.

"No, it's me. Just a quicky. I'm at the airport. I can see her now. She's not looking too good. We need some *Powidltascherl* and I need your help."

"We need some what?"

"Potato and plum dumplings, you know it, it's a Czech dish and..."

"OK, dad, I'm on it."

Monty kept the phone to his ear, confirming the ingredients and muttering affirmative sounds into the mouthpiece while watching Ingrid. She was giving a wide berth to the chattering groups of travellers exchanging information or flirting around the Christmas tree. For a person who simply had to know what was going on, Monty thought it odd that she eyed them with suspicion while rearranging her face into something that was casual and content.

"Yes, that's right. Italian prune plums," Monty said into the phone. "From the supermarket and in the foreign food section. Yes, see you in about thirty."

Monty switched off the phone and slid it into his pocket. Ingrid was worrying him. She was now smiling at everyone in a way that said, "Really, I am happy, really I am." But the nervous glances to right and left told Monty that, emotionally, Ingrid was all over the place.

Monty greeted her on the pavement and slipped her bag into the boot.

"Successful trip?" Monty asked, ushering her into the car.

Ingrid settled into the passenger seat, her head flicking round, and her eyes taking in everything. She leaned over and pecked Monty on the cheek.

"Yes, I would like you to answer your own question," Ingrid said again. "You can tell me whether or not the trip was worthwhile."

While the happy and chattering groups spilled out of the terminal and into the road, Ingrid leaned against the car door and gazed through the window at the tarmac. She removed her earrings and said:

"But you know, Monty, we should thank our lucky stars."

Monty switched on, the headlamps flickering into life and lighting up the road in front of them. He checked the rear-view mirror and indicated.

"Dementia is a terrible disease," Ingrid added.

Oh, God, so that was it.

Monty kept his reaction to himself. Pulling away from the kerbside, he knew that Ingrid was warming up, testing his presence; was Monty with her or not? They had barely left the quick-pick-up parking area when she said:

"On my way to Berlin I allowed myself to fantasize. I saw it all in my mind's eye: arriving at their house and finding it vibrant and buzzing. The children and grandchildren of the refugees would be sitting at the feet of their elders and listening to the old stories like I had listened to them. Open-mouthed we would wonder at the pictures they painted for us: the trek to Germany, all blankets, bedding and children snaking along the road to Germany, the curved backs of the old cast further down by suitcases and grief."

A slight throb in Monty's little toe reminded him just how heavy those wooden suitcases were. The one carried by Ingrid's grandparents contained Christmas decorations and used to live under the short flight of stairs leading to Julian's room. Recently, Ingrid had seen fit to relegate it to attic status. Out of sight meant out of mind. The next stage in the suitcase's history would be the rubbish dump.

"The sad thing is that the same picture would apply to the refugees coming up from Greece today," Ingrid said. "That bedding serves a double purpose: you sleep in it and you carry things in it. It's that simple."

And it was usually of good quality goose feathers, Monty thought. Seventy years later, Ingrid was still using the one she inherited from her grandmother.

"And can you imagine?" Ingrid said. "For much of that trek, there was the constant fear that they might be stopped by those who thought that there was nothing more fun than killing Germans."

Ingrid shook herself and appeared to be waking from a dream.

"Do you know, Monty?" she said, "they were not allowed to take more than 20 kilos with them? What is so special about the number "twenty" that makes it the standard weight? Even the airlines use that standard today. Why not twenty-one or twenty-three? Those extra figures actually meant items that had to be left behind."

They drove on in silence but Monty was watching her. Her eyes were on the city, blinking at its bright lights and tall buildings but she was not with him. She was at the core of herself. Monty supposed that the core of human beings did not die easily. It probably did not die at all. It was a place of habits, the habits of the child,

176

of being a child, and, in Ingrid's case, of being the child of refugees. When Monty had to brake sharply, the interruption shifted the mood in the car and Monty jumped in with a question before Ingrid could go back to her roots.

"So, if there was no family gathering, what did you see there?"

Ingrid reacted with a gasp of exasperation.

"When the door opened there was a stranger standing there, a stranger with a fading smile and clearly disappointed at seeing me at the door. I looked over his shoulder and into the house. It was dingy, cluttered, and I could smell beer and frying oil. The carpeted floor that I recalled was not carpeted at all. Our tables had been replaced by something that looked mass produced and there were children on the sofa and texting."

"So, in other words, this family was not your family or…"

Ingrid shook her head.

"No, no. I knew that after nearly 30 years they might have moved somewhere else. But it was the shock of seeing your memories revealed as a sham that was difficult to bear. The man must have seen my disappointment on my face and after a brief conversation he gave me an address. I thanked him and left."

"What about your brother?"

"Dieter? Didn't I tell you?"

"What didn't you tell me?"

"He moved to Dresden."

"No, you didn't tell me," Monty said trying to keep his voice free of accusation, irritation or hurt.

"Dieter has become a leading light in the *Pegida* movement. I have seen some of his posts on the *Pegida* website."

"I didn't know you had been looking at the *Pegida* website."

"Oh, yes, we want to know if attitudes to refugees have changed since 1946."

"We?"

"Yes, we at the VHS – at least those of us involved with refugees."

"And what have you found out? Have attitudes changed?"

He glanced at Ingrid's image in the windscreen. That image was shimmering in the reflection of the dashboard lights. Her eyes, lips and ears melted away as if at the command of an external force. Monty wondered whether she had heard his question. Eventually she said:

"Not a lot."

"Maybe," Monty said, decelerating behind a queue of brake lights, "victims of oppression, like Dieter, have it in them to create new victims themselves and then persecute them."

There was the touch of her hand alighting on Monty's wrist.

"I just want to go home now," Ingrid said. She looked at the line of trucks in front of them and added: "They didn't find another bomb, did they, Monty?"

There was a long period - the gestation period - Monty called it, in which neither of them said a word. They both tutted in frustration at the paper-chain of lights slung up the road in front of them and breathed sighs of relief when they reached the motorway. The car was doing around 120 when Ingrid said:

"I found mum and dad where the man told me - in a care home. They did not even recognize me at first."

Monty said nothing. There was nothing much to say when parents no longer recognize their own children.

"I told them my name," Ingrid said, "but they kept asking me who I was and why I had come. They both have varying degrees of dementia. They remember virtually nothing of the here and now. I wanted so much to tell them I forgave them for what they did. 'I forgive you,' I said, 'I forgive you,' but it didn't get through to them. Their memories seemed to have been wiped clean."

There was a long silence. Monty had used the same words just an hour earlier. Taking advantage of this trip to the airport, he had dropped into his office. Taking Lutz's computer and Lutz's phone from the boot of the car he had gone straight into the workshop and placed them on top of the other devices that were waiting to be doctored.

"Wipe the memories clean," he had said to his backroom employees.

"Shall I tell you the strangest thing?" Ingrid said.

Monty braked sharply and gesticulated an insult to a driver who had cut him up.

"Something about Kurt and Waltraud. Their childhood memories were as clear as crystal."

Monty changed up and accelerated quickly into the overtaking lane.

"I'm no expert," Monty said, "but I believe that is not unusual."

"Their memories of leaving their home in 1946 are still razor sharp. But I am not sure they knew who I was."

"Did they not give you some kind of sign that they knew you?"

The seat covering squeaked as Ingrid squirmed and cleared her throat.

"As I told you, Monty, I need you to tell me."

"Me, how can I…?"

"Pull over, Monty. I need to play you something."

"We're on a motorway, dear, and it is dark. We'll be home soon."

"Then we'll wait until then."

An abrupt silence.

"Talking of getting home, have you sorted your problems with Julian?"

Yes, their marriage was a successful work in progress but Monty was squirming in his seat. He was about to do something he had never done before. He was going to tell her a pack of lies.

"Actually," Monty said, "I had a bit a health scare while you were away."

22

Sunday – early evening

Monty was breathing more heavily than this simple comment on his health scare demanded. His heartbeat was now regular but he felt that something inside him had shifted. The old version of himself, the version he had created and lived with for more than 60 years, was slipping aside to make space for another Monty. The new version was already taking shape and telling him that the pursuit of righteousness belonged to the past. *That was a simpler era, Monty, when black was black and white was white.* Yes, Monty thought, being pragmatic was the name of the new game, rolling with the punches and staying on your feet. The year 2016 was on its way and it required a new and flexible approach to life, its joys and problems.

While Monty faced the task of adjusting his self-image, his breathing returned to normal and he settled in his seat.

"I was alright," he said while shaking his head. "It was just a dizzy spell and palpitations."

For Monty, the shaking head was a new departure, a

movement which he had once used to indicate ignorance but which he now appeared to be adopting in order to assuage doubts and to reassure. It did not appear to be working. Ingrid was looking sideways at him.

"Monty."

The falling intonation that accompanied the sound of his name was full of reproach and encouraged him to add:

"It's my age," he said. "Julian took me to the hospital and they did some tests."

"And?"

"It's called arrhythmia - a kind of irregular heartbeat. Nothing to worry about," Monty said.

"So, is that it?"

Monty hesitated, unsure whether he was using his health scare as a way of diverting Ingrid from her own disappointments or whether it was the former Monty and the pursuit of righteousness saying, "We have served you well - please don't let us go." The pursuit of righteousness was not giving up without a struggle and, after all, the old version of himself had lived by its dictum that hiding vital information was as good as telling lies.

Monty pictured himself in the basement of Lutz's house. He was frantic and pouring petrol over the floor. He did not see Julian in his memory but Monty knew his son had been there. At the time, possessed by inner demons, Monty had shown no restraint. Nobody and nothing was going to stop him from splashing the liquid over the walls and ceiling of the coal room and throwing the can to one side. The truth was that when he had lit the wick of the petrol bomb, he had given no thought to the fact that he was about to put his life and those of the other people in the Villa Rosa in danger. He was on auto pilot and acting to some prearranged plan already written out in detail.

"Yes, that's it," Monty said. "They will want to do more tests but they assure me there is nothing to worry about."

It was the shortness of breath and slight chest pain that had worried the doctors. He told them that he had been in the garden, had seen smoke coming from the neighbour's house when he fell to the floor in distress.

"If it hadn't been for Julian…," Monty said.

If it had not been for Julian, Monty might have considered going to the police and telling them what really happened in Lutz's house. But Julian had convinced him to tell neither the doctors nor the Police.

"Nobody else needs to know," Julian added.

And Julian persuaded his father to include Ingrid in "nobody else." They were not covering anything up, Julian said. Their decision was humane and pragmatic and one that would save Ingrid a good deal of unnecessary concern.

"Then we'd better make a plan," Ingrid said. "A plan to get you back to your normal self."

"Normal self?"

"Yes, your normal self. And we'll start with a cup of tea. Then I will play you a recording I made of Kurt and Waltraud. They were talking about their experiences as refugees. I want you to tell me. From what you hear, do you think they recognized me or not?"

Monty swung off the motorway at the *Tannenheim* exit and followed his headlamps in the direction of the town centre. He and Ingrid had always prided themselves on their honesty and he longed to tell her the exciting news that he had changed, moved on, left the old Monty with his "normal self" behind.

"I'll be fine," said Monty. "Look at me. I'm as fit as a fiddle."

But he had not been as fit as a fiddle 12 hours previously. It was the speed of events that had proved too much for Monty. While he lay prostrate on the floor, unable to stand or breathe easily, Julian had been the hero. Without Julian, Monty might never have got out of Lutz's house alive. Without Julian they would never have escaped with the incriminating evidence.

Monty had a vague recollection of Julian stuffing Lutz's phone into his pocket and the computer into the hood of his sweater. He felt Julian fumbling around his back before being raised to his feet by a powerful lift of Julian's legs. Next, Julian grabbed Monty's right hand and draped it over his shoulder before lifting his father off his feet and carrying him out of the house.

"I tell you one thing, Monty."

It was Ingrid. She had edged closer while Monty drove into *Tannenheim* and up the main street.

"I shall take special care of you," she said.

"I'm fine. It was just a heart scare."

Neither Monty nor Julian had known that when Julian carefully placed his father on the path near the dividing picket fence. Monty was free of chest flutters, free of confusion and giddiness but his hands were trembling. It was still dark and yet he saw plumes of smoke squeezing through the basement windows. From somewhere far away there were shouts. He recognised the voices of Herr Vorberg the baker and his neighbour from across the street, Mizzi Maier. He heard Mizzi scream:

"Call the Fire Brigade."

There had been another voice in his ear and Julian appeared, sweeping away soil from the path.

"Stick to the concrete paths," Julian had said. "Better not to leave footprints."

Monty changed down to second to take the corner that led into his street. The presence of the emergency service vehicles registered immediately. Nearly 60 years previously, the sight of such vehicles by the smoking garages in Long Ditton village had brought such guilt to

Monty's shoulders that he had confessed to the police. His confession had saved Nigel and Steffi Cole from taking the blame. In 2016, the new Monty felt no guilt and had no intention of going to the police and blurting out, "It was me." In that moment, as he approached his house, the old Monty finally let go of the pursuit of righteousness and the new Monty took charge. He could not even be bothered to turn his head and bid his old companion farewell.

"Now Monty, when we get home, I want you to sit down, have a cup of tea and listen to my recording. I need your opinion."

But Monty was only half-listening to his wife. Her words reminded him of Julian's voice from 10 hours previously.

"I want you to sit down, dad, rest and then we need to clean you up and get you to hospital."

The hospital's on-duty doctor was an Australian and working in Germany on an exchange year. After a few tests, he said:

"It's arrhythmia."

He concluded that Monty's heart was fundamentally sound for a man of his age but that he needed a reset. He had even attempted a joke as he attached special paddles to Monty's chest.

"New heart means a new man. I should be so lucky."

Before he could comment, Monty was asleep and the doctor was delivering electric shocks through the paddles on his chest in order to regularise his heartbeat. Monty scratched at the skin where the paddles had touched it. He had been told to constantly monitor himself, but Monty reckoned he had got off lightly.

There was an intake of breath from the passenger seat.

"Look, Monty," Ingrid said, pointing at the flashing lights of the emergency vehicles. "Something's going on at the Villa Rosa. Look there."

Monty leaned forward and stared through the windscreen. Now was testing time. His opinion of Ingrid's recording would have to wait a little longer.

23

Sunday – early evening

Ingrid's sharp breath suggested surprise but she managed to infuse the word "look" not only with disgust, but also with a tone which, to Monty, suggested a confirmation of long-held suspicions and fears.

"Well, what a surprise," she said. "Peter Lutz is in trouble."

She shook her head.

"So, Monty, you'd better tell me all about how the police found out about this individual and arrested him."

Monty looked sideways and into the dark stillness of an early-Sunday-evening pavement. He said:

"Have they arrested him?"

Ingrid shrugged.

"I don't know. I've been away, remember? Are you sure you're alright, Monty?"

Monty nodded.

"Please tell me what happened, Monty."

Ingrid's tone was gentle rather than scolding but Monty knew there was no point in arguing.

"It happened very early this morning."

"It? What is 'it'?"

"The fire," Monty said. "The whole house could've gone up. Fortunately, they managed to put it out. I think there was some kind of blaze in the basement."

That Sunday morning had indeed been disturbed by sirens blaring and blue lights illuminating the most secret corners of the street and making its inhabitants pull on their collective trousers. The two cars now parked outside the Villa Rosa were a mere reminder of the whining and the flashing that had responded to Mizzi Maier's request and disturbed them all only 12 hours before. Through the glass frontage of his sitting-room, Monty had seen that sacred space of early morning sleep swept aside and trampled over by huge firemen, bellowed orders and hauled hoses. Standing by the drinks table, Monty imagined he saw disappointment behind the masks that covered the firemen's faces. Despite the sound and fury, this was, after all, just a small fire in a basement and easily brought under control.

"Some kind of blaze? Don't you know exactly what happened?" Ingrid said. "Why didn't you ask?"

Monty turned though their gates, his headlamps sweeping over the driveway. He switched off the engine, touched at his nose and sniffed.

"Because I was most of the morning at the hospital," he said.

Ingrid opened the car door, swung her feet out and rested them on the gravelled driveway. She lifted her hand to her chin and stroked it. She might have been mocking him when she said over her shoulder.

"You are not deaf and blind, Monty. You must have seen and heard something."

Monty shook his head, took another silent breath and ran his fingers through his big hair. Ingrid was insistent.

"Come on, Monty. When did you notice something

was wrong?"

"Not until I came downstairs this morning. Actually, I was hoping to speak to people in the street so I went outside to clear away leaves when I started to have trouble with my breathing."

For several seconds neither of them spoke. Both heard the ongoing investigation from the Villa Rosa. The investigators' voices were calm, cold, and masterful and a suitable backdrop to Monty's reflections on the ease of lying. He did not at first notice that Ingrid had half-turned and was looking sideways at him and barely nodding to herself when she said:

"I see."

Her voice was tight and controlled and Monty noticed that Ingrid's eyes, dark and solemn, were wandering. He was too astonished at the absence of angry prefects to reflect on the ripple of muscle around her mouth. The ripple might have been the beginning of a smile. It could equally have been the start of a grimace or a scowl. Monty considered neither of these possibilities. He was thanking his lucky stars that there were no thunderbolts hurtling in his direction, a gift from a heavenly body intent on punishing him for his "pragmatic" explanation.

Ingrid leaned forward and got out of the car with a push of the thighs. She strolled back to the gate and Monty watched as she half disappeared into the darkness before reappearing in the light from the street lamp. She peeped down the street and drew her head back as though a bee had flown too close to her nose. She hurried back to the car.

"There are people walking about," Ingrid said in a stage whisper.

Monty pushed at the car door and swung out. At that moment, Herr Maier, his "Sunday best" still hanging loosely on his frame, rushed across the road and stopped in the lamplight by the front gate. His wife's presence was signalled by her heels clickety-clacking on the road several paces behind him. Eventually, she arrived, tottering into the light and grabbing at her husband's arm. Monty barely had time to decide whether or not she had taken one or two "drops" too many when Herr Maier said:

"Herr Brodnitz - what is going on in the garden? Do you know?"

Monty mumbled some reply, embarrassed by Herr Maier's use of his surname in combination with the informal "*du*" rather than the formal "*Sie.*" He blew out his cheeks and, wondering if the novelty and excitement of the events had resulted in a breakthrough in their neighbourly relationship, he said:

"I'm really not sure, Herr Maier."

While the others watched the dark shapes and torchlight of the men circling the Villa Rosa, Monty examined Mizzi Maier. Unstable on her heels, she was holding on to her husband as if he were her lifeline. The light, shining on her coiffure, cast strange shadows onto her face and turned it into something resembling a Halloween dummy. He said:

"I suppose they must be the fire investigators."

Occasionally the investigators stopped to point at something and wrote in their notebooks. The torchlight suggested that they were concentrating on the basement windows and the bricked-up coal hole. He was sure that he saw flame-shaped soot marks licking up the side of the house and bearing witness to the fact that the fire might have destroyed the entire house had the sprinkler system not worked and the fire services not been alerted.

"Do they know how it started, Herr Brodnitz?"

Monty shook his head.

"No idea, I'm afraid, Herr Maier. Perhaps an electrical fault?"

He was delighted to see that the others took his

comment as absent-mindedly as it had been made. Ingrid nodded and said:

"A short circuit, yes. I'm sure you're right, Monty."

"But I don't know for sure. It's just a guess really."

"Of course, Monty."

"I don't think so," Mizzi said, coming alive from under her husband's arm. "Herr Lutz recently had his house rewired."

"Shoddy workmanship, then?" Monty said.

"Not by Germans," Herr Maier said.

"Then who was it, Wolfi?"

Monty stepped forward and stood at Mizzi Maier's shoulder. Her Mascara had smudged and the rouge on her cheeks looked like clown make-up and by now she was well out of her husband's shadow.

"Well, Wolfi," Mizzi said, "who was it? Poles? Turks? Perhaps some poor refugee who managed to find a job? Anyone but your perfect Germans, eh?"

Monty cleared his throat into the uncomfortable silence.

"I'm sure these men will find the cause," he said.

"Let's hope so," Ingrid said. "Where is the owner?"

"I thought you said he'd been arrested," Monty said.

"The man deserves to be," Ingrid said.

Ingrid never used Peter's name. When Monty had told her about his collection, Peter ceased to exist for her. She stripped him of his identity, his humanity and he became a mere thing - an owner, that man, that person.

"We have heard rumours that it was arson," Herr Maier said.

Ingrid turned around.

"Really?"

"So I am told."

"By whom?"

Monty took a deep breath, swirled his hand around in

the air and shrugged.

"They are just rumours," he said. "You know, things that circulate and..."

"Yes, I know what 'rumours' are, Monty. So, it is likely that the fire was deliberate?"

Coldly and efficiently were words Monty could have added. The clarity of his focus in the cellar had been something he had rarely experienced in life but getting his hands on the computer and phone required tunnel vision. Nothing else had been of the slightest importance - not even damage to property or people.

"Rumours say," Herr Maier said, "that the fire was started by Peter Lutz."

"I always thought the man was a psychopath," Ingrid said.

"Rumour also has it that he needed the insurance money," Mizzi said, tottering on her heels. "The house and collection are insured for huge sums."

"All that Nazi nonsense insured?" Ingrid said. "It's obscene. I was under the impression that trade in Nazi antiquities is banned in Germany."

"It is," Monty said. "But it is not banned throughout the world. The market is enormous."

"Disgusting," Ingrid commented.

Herr Maier looked at his wife and raised an eyebrow. Mizzi Maier nodded and her husband said:

"There is also speculation that the fire was the excuse the police needed to get their hands on the man known as the *Sturmbannfuehrer*."

While Monty stared at the ground, Ingrid took a deep breath and fixed her eyes on the Villa Rosa. Her mouth remained open while she raised her hands to cup her cheeks. Her surprise made for a breathy response, a whispered question rather than a demand wrapped up in question marks.

"Are you telling me that that unpleasant individual

was actually Peter Lutz?"

Herr Maier nodded a "yes" and simultaneously tutted his feelings about it.

"I suppose they could get him for incitement to violence."

"And we've been living next door to a maniac," Mizzi said. "The man is a disgrace and he's not even a Turk or a Pole. He's German."

There were shouts of excitement from the garden of the Villa Rosa. Monty looked into the darkness but saw nobody. The shouts came again. Maybe the investigators had wandered into the old stables at the back of the house and discovered more examples of Lutz's guilty secret.

"Then God help him," Ingrid said. "He'll have to live with guilt for the rest of his life."

Monty winced. He felt no guilt with regard to Lutz but lifelong guilt was something he knew about. This was guilt as self-sabotage, guilt as poison that killed the mind and spirit, guilt that kept him in a past he could do nothing about.

You refused to accept your dad's choice of partner, didn't you, Monty? You did not even go to Ashley's funeral. You were not there when your dad passed away. You were not really there when he was alive. And you say that you adored your dad? You have invented memories for yourself, my boy.

One day, his father had said:

"Of course, you know Ashley and I are a couple, don't you, Monty?"

Monty recalled that he had not immediately reacted. Inside his world was falling apart. He left for the university next day and cried like a little boy. He had nothing against the idea of homosexuality but it was not what he wanted in a father. Monty continued to visit his dad but there were tensions. Some topics were avoided when they met. And because he could not mention a gay father to his friends, he felt he had lost him. He continued to hope that his dad would one day meet Mrs Right and come back to him. But that day never came.

Herr Maier took a step forward and took his wife's elbow.

"I'm sure the police will fix everything," he said to Ingrid.

He then muttered something in his wife's ear and wished the "Brodnitz family" a good evening before Mizzi set her hand on her man's shoulder and tottered off across the road and into the night.

"And have you fixed your problems?" Ingrid said.

"Which ones?"

"Your problems with Julian."

"We're working on it."

"Don't give up, Monty."

Give up? You don't have a good track record, Monty.

"I won't give up," he said.

"How are you going about it?"

"Facing it," said Monty.

"And?"

"By talking."

"About?"

There was a slight shift in Monty's expression.

"About Julian's sexuality," he said, acknowledging that the word "homosexual" still did not come easily to his lips. He and Julian had broached the subject late on Friday night. Neither of them had noticed midnight come and go as they plunged headlong towards a new dawn. But Monty knew that "new dawns" were elusive things and not given to clear beginnings and clear endings. He also knew that, like many fathers, he had failed to see that his child had slipped through his fingers and become an adult. He was now grateful to Julian for

194

having saved his life. Wimbledon Grammar School for Boys would have been proud of him.

"Are you OK, Monty?"

"I'm fine."

"Only you're so pale."

"I'm OK, really."

"Really? We need to take care of you, Monty. Let's go inside."

Slipping her arm into his, the two of them approached the front door and entered the house. Closing the door behind him Monty said:

"I have a surprise for you."

"I love surprises but why didn't you tell me?"

"What kind of logic is that?" Julian said from the kitchen.

Monty led his wife into the glass-fronted sitting-room, placed his hands on her shoulders and guided her onto a chair.

"Julian and I decided to make you something from your childhood."

Julian slipped a plate onto a side table, stepped backwards and stood shoulder to shoulder with his father.

"It's something your mother might have made you when you were a child," Monty added. "*Böhmische Knödel* - 'potato plum dumplings' in English."

"You made it?"

"We made it," Julian said.

Ingrid opened her mouth to reply but the thumping roar of a pack of motorbikes broke the peace and quiet of the house. Monty watched the burly, helmeted riders pass by his house. Ingrid was about to speak when Monty's attention was stolen from him. The leader, all shiny black leather and military helmet, caught Monty's eye, held it for several seconds before accelerating away.

"You are such a bad liar, Monty. But don't be hard

on yourself," Ingrid said. "Sometimes the end justifies the means."

She reached for her handbag and pulled out a mobile phone.

"Now, boys, listen to this. It's a recording I made of my mum and dad yesterday."

She put the phone on the table between them.

"Nobody had a mobile device in the care home," Ingrid said. "The only electronic squeaks you heard there were the ones that told nurses someone wanted the toilet."

Then, she pushed the play button.

24

Sunday – early evening

There were a few voices, old voices, revealing a number of German regional accents that Monty was unable to recognise. There were other voices, foreign voices, betraying the nationalities of the speakers, nurses perhaps, calling out names that had long since gone out of fashion: Hildegard, Frieda, Adolf, Heinz and Erwin. A telephone rang, a cup rattled on its saucer. It was a reminder to Monty that life in this home was another era preserved, and he put faces to the redundant names and imagined them talking about jobs that no longer existed, ice cutter, lamplighter or lift man. He sensed both the joy and the inertia of the place but nothing could compensate for the home's unspoken function: a place where elderly people were left by their families to die.

Then, there was Ingrid, her voice animated and loud.

"Tell us about what happened to you in 1946, Waltraud."

"I was a child - 10 years old - and 1946 was the year we left home," Waltraud said, her voice shaking and crackling with tremors.

"Tell me what happened to you."

"Suddenly we were all awake to shouting and banging at the front door."

"Who was at the door, Waltraud?" Ingrid asked.

"I ran to the window. I was thinking it was the Russians again. I shouted: 'What is it? What do you want?' The answer came from a Czech patrol."

"What did the patrol want, Waltraud?"

"I ran down the steps and opened the door. I was given a shove so I ran up the steps again. A Czech soldier with wild hair broke into our house and, with his gun at the ready, he cracked a whip."

"What did this man do?"

"Long hair, for that is what I called him, shouted: 'Fast, faster: it is already 1:30 AM and you should have been in the square at midnight. Did you not hear the message on the loudspeaker?' I said 'No'. Long hair cracked his whip and with his gun he pointed at me. In 10 minutes, we had to be ready. In 10 minutes, we had to be ready to leave. I asked long hair what was going to happen to us. 'You will find that out quickly. Don't take much with you - only a piece of bread.'

Can you imagine how I felt? Can you imagine how frightened my mother was? If only my daddy had been there. But he had been killed by the Russians. My mother and I, we poor souls, had nothing."

"So, what did you take?" Ingrid said.

"We wretches could not take much with us. My mother grabbed a few photos of my dear father and stuffed them into my rucksack. I also stuffed in a small pillow, a blanket, and one set of clothing. Then my mother grabbed daddy's pension plan and the inheritance documents of the house but everything else had to remain behind. Everything else! That was the only thought that flashed in my mind. The savages then drove us out of our home into the street and then to the town square. The streets were already empty but on the town square they already had people standing in rows of five and we were the last ones to join them under a barrage of cursing, whipping and pushes with gun butts. Cursing and whipping and gun butts..."

"What was going on there?" Ingrid prompted.

"What did we see there? Our dear citizens, young and old, the sick in wheelchairs, the old and weak, some with knapsacks over their shoulders or suitcases. Most were like us, without anything. Others were in underclothes and some had nothing left and had to appear wrapped in a linen cloth. If only my daddy had been there. He would have stopped long hair when he came. Long hair came and took away my mum's last possessions. He took away her bankbook, her house keys and her jewellery! The other brave and honourable citizens suffered no less.

By then the first rays of the rising sun appeared on the horizon. It was 4.00 o'clock in the morning, and the wretched column of people was set in motion with lashes of dog whips, gun butts and curses. We proceeded down Linden Strasse. When passing *Cillich Strasse* I gave a furtive glance at the house of my dear friend Gustav and prayed to God he would protect him. The poor boy did not know that his sister Helli and many of his dear school friends were being deported. Nor did he hear my lamentations and cries. I did not shed a tear. I only felt hate in my heart for these evil Czech people. I did not even turn to say, 'God will pay you back.'

So moved this suffering train of humanity. Five thousand people left, within 10 minutes, as beggars. We were thrown out, out of our home, our beloved *Neutitschein*, our jewel..."

"Thank you, Waltraud," Ingrid said and the she addressed her father.

"Kurt?"

"I was 12 years old," he said, the voice thin and

breathy. "My mum and dad and I arrived in *Zauchtel* completely drenched. Even the heavens cried over us unfortunate wretches. We were loaded onto open coal-railroad cars, seventy to seventy-five people to each car, plus baby carriages and the remaining belongings. Some families, who were separated in the camp, were reunited here, but most people remained alone, looking for their dear ones but without success. Children cried, looking for their parents and not knowing that they languished in prison. In the coal car with me, I found several acquaintances: Frau Weiss with her mother, Roswitha; Frau Lippert and her daughters, Anni and Sabina; Frau Krauss, Frau Uchtdorf, Frau Fink, Frau Glotz, and many others. My friend Mizzi Wirth sat next to us in the car and cried for her mother. She didn't know. But how could I tell her mother had committed suicide?

It rained continuously; the doors of the railroad cars were then closed and before long we were drenched to the skin as nobody carried an umbrella and the cars were not covered. At 8.00 o'clock everything was ready for the transport and how we rushed! In a fast ride we went through *Prerau, Olmuetz, Truebau* and at midnight we arrived at *Kolin*. Without food I cried out from hunger and cold. Everything was soaking wet. To relieve yourself you had to do it in the cars, and the cars were not opened throughout the entire trip.

At last we arrived in Germany and the camp at *Pirna*. There had been an outbreak of Hunger typhus there and mummy died of it in this camp. The camp was overcrowded. It was too small and new refugees were added hourly. In the meadows and ditches there were none but poor wretched creatures, we beggars made homeless by the Germans in Germany, treated as lepers. Not even a glass of water was given to us without being asked the question: 'Why did you come here? Why did you not stay there with the Czechs?' Our explanation that we were evacuated and robbed by the Czechs only provoked stubborn silence. That was always a slap in the face and we would walk away sadly. When dad and me eventually arrived in Berlin, the view of it we could have done without. Berlin! You beautiful city! Only a sea of stones..."

"Thank you," Ingrid said.

Silence.

"Thank you," Ingrid repeated.

Monty heard a sound. It must have been Kurt stifling a sob.

"Dascha, dascha," he said.

Monty looked at Ingrid. She put a finger to her lips and a hand over his. Something wet fell on Monty's forearm.

"Daschund, daschund."

Monty looked up as Kurt made a final effort and breathed out in triumph.

"Danke schoen, danke schoen, danke schoen..."

A few more wet drops splashed onto Monty's hand. He and Ingrid had been together for 23 years.

"Danke schoen, Ingrid, danke schoen."

But he had never seen her cry.

Printed in Great Britain
by Amazon